She loved Guy, but she knew if she stayed with him, people would shun him too…

The one who started coming between Lorraine and Guy was Amy and an older woman who looked like she could be her mother.

That woman sure looks familiar. Where do I know her from? Oh no, it can't be her.

Lorraine remembered a prison guard who was especially nasty. Suddenly, she started shaking. She went to the bathroom to compose herself.

While she was there, the older woman entered. She gave Lorraine an intense look and, with false sweetness, said, "The colors of black and white suit you a lot better than orange. You can't fool me. I know you from Perryville. I know you are a murderer. They should have never let you out."

Lorraine stared at the woman with her mouth open. She could not utter a sound.

"You damn black widow spider, how can you trap Guy in your net? He is way too good for the likes of you. I hope you rot in hell."

Lorraine Albright Lopez is released from an Arizona prison after serving fifteen years for killing her husband in self-defense. She is now thirty-seven and has three children who have been alienated against her by her husband's parents who have custody of them. Bitter and resentful of her in-laws, whose money and power had her incarcerated when she should have gone free, Lorraine decides to leave Arizona in a used RV and start a new life on the road. But her in-laws want her dead and will stop at nothing to achieve this. Can Lorraine put her past behind her and start over, or will the mistakes she made when she was young and foolish haunt for the rest of her life—however long, or short, that may be?

KUDOS for *Released*

In *Released* by Ellynore Seybold-Smith, Lorraine Lopez kills her abusive husband in self-defense, but because of her in-laws power, money, and influence, she is sentenced to 15 years in prison. When she gets out, she wants to start a new life, but her troubles are not yet behind her. Someone is out to kill her—most likely, her in-laws—and she is forced to flee her home state of Arizona in a used motorhome to start a new life on the road. Even there, her past comes back to haunt her, threatening to destroy the new life she has created and the new love she has found. Seybold-Smith writes a touching tale of second-chance love and forgiveness with charming characters and real-life experiences that makes you think the author has been there and knows what she is talking about. ~ *Taylor Jones, Reviewer*

Released by Ellynore Seybold-Smith is a contemporary romance with a darker side. Our heroine, Lorraine Albright Lopez, gets pregnant at seventeen and has to marry her boyfriend Alex, who turns out to be an abusive pervert. When he attacks Lorraine and she is forced to defend herself, it is a clear case of self-defense. However, Alex's parents are very wealthy and have a lot of influence in Lorraine's home town of Yuma, Arizona. And Lorraine's parents are strictly lower middle class. Her public defender attorney is no match for Alex's parents' influence, and Lorraine is convicted and sentenced to fifteen years in prison. When she gets out, her father is dead, her three children—who have been in the custody of Alex's parents—want nothing to do with her, and someone starts taking pot shots at her, trying to kill her. Knowing that there is nothing for her in Yuma anymore, Lorraine buys a used RV and takes to the road to start a new life and leave her past behind her. But she discovers, much to her dismay, that her past won't stay put that easily. *Released* is a poignant and heart-warming story of second chances, courage, and the scars that domestic abuse can leave on its innocent victims. Seybold-Smith has constructed a good solid plot with endearing and intriguing characters that tug at your heartstrings. *~ Regan Murphy, Reviewer*

ACKNOWLEDGEMENTS

This book was written because I signed up for NaNoWriMo, and the challenge was to write 50,000 words in one month. I never believed I could do it but, to my own surprise, I did, and actually wrote a story. It took me a few more weeks to write the ending.

I want to thank the wonderful staff at Black Opal Books for accepting my submission and working with me as if I was the only writer they dealt with. From the times I get e-mails, I don't think Lauri Wellington ever sleeps.

Writing can be a lonely profession, but I appreciate all my fellow writer friends who encouraged me. Thank you, Write on the Edge Yuma, and Pinkie Paranya.

Released

Ellynore Seybold-Smith

A Black Opal Books Publication

Black Opal Books

BECAUSE SOME STORIES JUST HAVE TO BE TOLD

GENRE: CONTEMPORARY ROMANCE/WOMEN'S FICTION/ROMANTIC SUSPENSE

This is a work of fiction. Names, places, characters and incidents are either the product of the author's imagination or are used fictitiously, and any resemblance to any actual persons, living or dead, businesses, organizations, events or locales is entirely coincidental. All trademarks, service marks, registered trademarks, and registered service marks are the property of their respective owners and are used herein for identification purposes only. The publisher does not have any control over or assume any responsibility for author or third-party websites or their contents.

DEDICATION

This book is dedicated to all victims of abuse.

Chapter 1

The horrible sound of the steel bars closing was suddenly like sweet music. Now it was the music of release. Everyone looked at Lorraine Lopez as she walked past their cells.

"Good bye, gringo."

"Good luck out there, Lori."

"Say hello to the sunshine for me."

"We'll see you in six months or so. You'll be back."

No, never will I be back. I will make it. I will not return to this hell hole.

In a dressing room, she opened the bag of clothes her brother had brought her. There was a pair of black cotton slacks and a soft, silky tunic with many colors and some sequins. She put it on and looked in the mirror. "Wow, how beautiful. I will never wear the color orange again."

Outside, she met her brother, Frank Albright. After the lengthy hug, she looked at his face and saw tears in his eyes.

"Sis, good seeing you again. Mom didn't come. She wants to have a nice dinner ready when you get home."

Home, I'm going home. Oh, Lord, thank you, thank you, thank you.

They went to get her belongings, a watch that was not running, a golden wedding band, an engagement ring with a one carat diamond, a golden cross on a chain, pearl stud earrings, and a set of keys.

"And here is the money you had in your bank account. You've accumulated quite a nice nest egg," said the paymaster.

"Thank you, and good bye."

Frank and Lorraine stepped into the sunshine as the heavy metal door shut behind them.

She looked at the blue clear sky and took a deep breath of the clean March air.

"Free, free at last. Oh God, I'm free at last."

"The car is right over there, Lori."

"Lori was the little girl from the past. Now I am Lorraine, Brother."

"Whatever you say, Sis."

Frank opened a silver Dodge minivan, put in her small duffel bag while she took a seat on the passenger side. "Nice car, what year is it?"

"A 2016, you like it?"

"Yeah, the chariot taking me into freedom. Get those horses moving to Yuma."

"You want radio?" he asked.

"No, Frank, silence is golden. Just hearing your voice is music enough."

"You know I'm not much of a talker while driving."

As they drove through the desert Lorraine enjoyed looking at every bush and saguaro cactus and every tree struggling in the harsh environment. Soon her thoughts went back, back to the time when she was young and innocent. A time past with so many mistakes. If only she had known then what she knew now was the prevailing thought.

c∕∂c∕∂

Twenty years earlier:

"Lori, you ready to go?"

Lorraine heard her friend Kimberly calling up the steps of the small craftsman house in the old section of Yuma, Arizona.

"Yeah, I'll be right down."

One last check in the mirror was satisfactory. She was proud of the look she gave to her jeans. Plain fifteen dollar jeans were updated with appliques of lace, giving them an expensive boutique look. Two foam pads cut out of an old dress of her mother's added the just needed amount of padding to make her cleavage visible in her red shirt. Her brown hair spilled over her shoulders in large curls. *Amazing how a little color on the eyelids make the eyes look so much larger.* A trace of red lipstick gave her face a glow.

She went downstairs and stood the scrutiny of her mother after pulling up the neckline of her shirt as far as she could.

"You pass. Now you two girls enjoy the rodeo. I'm expecting you back for supper. Of course you are invited too, Kimberly."

"Thank you, Mrs. Albright. We'll be back as soon as the rodeo is over. May Lori go to the dance with me tonight?"

"You girls looking to pick up some cowboys?"

"Just to dance with," Kimberly said. "Maybe Frank can go too."

"I don't know what his plans are. He'll be home for supper."

"Good," said Kimberly with a smile.

As the girls headed toward the little Honda parked at the curb, Lorraine said, "You sure are lucky to have a car. It's too far to walk to the fairground."

"Yeah, my father gave it to me. Since my parents divorced, they are competing with each other for my love. Mother buys me nice clothes. Father buys me a used car. When I get mad at Mom, I threaten to live with Dad. It works. I can do what I want, get showered with gifts. Maybe you should wish for your parents to get divorced."

"Doubt that would work for me. I do love both my mom and dad and I'm glad they get along."

At the fairground, they sat in the bleachers near where the contestants entered. Soon three Mexican men took the seats next to them. The young man next to Lori was about an inch taller than her five feet seven inches. He had the most handsome face Lorraine had ever seen.

He smiled at both girls. "*Buenos tardes.*"

"*Buenos tardes,*" the girls replied.

"Oh, you speak Spanish."

"Yes, two years in high school and the rest practice with friends," Lorraine replied as she looked deep into his brown eyes.

He returned the look by staring into her face as if she was the most beautiful girl he had ever seen. Suddenly no one else existed around them.

"My name is Alexandro Lopez. But everybody calls me Alex."

"I'm Lori Albright."

"Nice to meet you, Miss Albright."

"Please, call me Lori." Feeling a nudge from Kimberly, she said, "and this is my friend Kimberly."

"And these are my friends Jose and Ricardo, known as Dick."

"Nice to meet you," the girls said. "Been to the rodeo before?"

"Oh yes, we go every year. We live in Yuma," Alex said. "I hope to see more of you, Lori."

"I'm going to the dance tonight."

"I am too," Alex said enthusiastically. "You boys going, too?"

"Yea," said Dick, "I'm bringing my girlfriend."

"I don't have a girlfriend to bring," Alex said. "I'd be delighted to meet you there."

"Since you don't have a girlfriend to bring, does that mean you have one you cannot bring?"

"No, it means I don't have a girlfriend. Maybe that is about to change," he said, giving Lorraine a very intense look.

I can't believe this. This very handsome man interested in little old me. He could have a million girls swooning over him. What does he see in me? Maybe he's an illegal looking for an American wife? How can I ask if he is legal without seeming too prying?

"You lived in Yuma long?"

"All my life," he said proudly.

"You were born here, well so was I."

"I knew we had a lot in common."

Their conversation ended abruptly when the announcer started the beginning of the rodeo. Everyone stood for the prayer and the singing of "The Star Spangled Banner." Then the rodeo queen with her court rode in on horses decorated with glitter on their flanks. The afternoon was peppered with loud enthusiastic cheers.

After one cowboy got a good time roping a calf, Alex turned to Lori. "That's my cousin."

"Wonderful." And she gave an extra loud cheer.

When the rodeo was over, Alex turned to the two girls. "Hope to see you at the dance tonight. Please save a dance for me, Lori."

"I think I can manage that. See you later."

She watched the boys walk in the other direction. Alex turned around and gave her a friendly wave, then walked with his friends to another section of the parking lot.

"Lori, I see your cheeks are red and it's not only from the sun. You look like you're in love."

"Kim, I think I am. I really don't know what being in love feels like. In all my seventeen years I have never felt like this. Do you think it's love? This feeling is inside me all the way to my crotch."

"Girlfriend, you better not talk like that around your mother."

"You bet I won't. That's why I talk like that to you."

"That's what girlfriends are for."

"Have you ever seen a better looking man in your life? I wonder how old he is."

"I would say about twenty. When you see him again, and I'm sure you will, just ask him."

"I'll do that. Oh I sure hope he shows up tonight. Do you think I'm pretty enough for him?"

"He seems to think so. Lori, I don't know why you think you're not pretty. You have nice hair."

"A mousy brown,"

"You have lovely hazel eyes."

"With short lashes."

"Yeah, but you can buy long lashes."

"With my mother? She would ground me for a month."

"Your lips are pretty full and kissable."

"How would you know they're kissable?"

"Just a guess. You've got nice teeth."

"They should be. My parents paid enough for braces. But then there's my nose. Do you think I should get a nose job?"

"Girl, there is nothing wrong with your nose. It fits your face."

"I wish it was smaller with a little uplift like yours."

"I have to be so careful that I show no buggers. Lori, you have to think pretty. Stand in front of the mirror and say I am pretty, I am beautiful. Tell yourself that until you believe it."

"Is that what you do?"

"Not anymore."

It took a good fifteen minutes for them to get out of the parking lot and slowly through heavy traffic on Thir-ty-Second Street before they got onto Fourth Avenue to-ward home.

When they arrived at the Albright house, Mr. Albright and Frank were sitting on the porch drinking beer.

"Hello girls, have a good time at the rodeo?" called Mr. Albright.

"Yes Daddy, it was so much fun," she said, giving her father a hug. "Hello, Frank, you have a good day?

"Great, sold a car."

"Super, how many is that this month?"

"Three so far, and the month is still young."

"You going to the dance tonight?" Kimberly asked,

"Yeah, I'll be glad to take both of you girls."

Kimberly smiled, giving Frank a hopeful look. "Great,"

I wonder if Kim is really my friend or if I'm just a means for her to get close to Frank. One never knows who is really a friend.

Mrs. Albright appeared at the door. "Supper's ready. You all go and wash up."

"We know to wash our hands," Frank said.

"Mother's said that phrase for so long, I don't think she could say *supper's ready* without that appendage," Mr. Albright commented. Over the dinner the only conversation was the rodeo and their hope for the upcoming dance. "We'll go tomorrow afternoon, won't we, Lorne?" Mrs. Albright asked her husband.

"Yes, Mary, it's Saturday when I always have a date with my favorite girl," Mr. Albright said, giving his wife a loving look.

She smiled and proceeded to take a bite of salmon.

"Good dinner as usual," said Frank.

"Thank you, Frank."

"Yes, very good, Mrs. Albright," Kimberly agreed. "Usually I don't like fish, but when you make it, it's delicious."

She's lying, thought Lori. *She just wants Frank to notice her.*

"Can I help you with the dishes?" Kimberly asked.

"Thanks for the offer, Kim, but I'll have the dishwasher loaded in no time. If you want to help me clear the table…"

"Sure, then I have to go home and get ready for the dance. Will you pick me up at my house, Frank?"

"Yeah, I'll be by at 7:30, how's that?"

"Fine, I'll be ready. Thank you again for supper, Mrs. Albright. Hope to see you at the rodeo tomorrow then."

"Glad you could join us. Have a good time at the dance. Bye."

Kimberly waved as she headed out the door. "Bye."

"Nice girl, and pretty too." Mrs. Albright said.

There, that's Mom's way of saying that I'm not pretty.

"I'm going for a little walk before I need to get dressed for the dance."

"You don't have much time. Don't you want to take a shower and get ready?" Mom asked.

"I got my clothes laid out. I can be showered and dressed in twenty minutes."

"Okay, don't get lost."

"I don't think so. I've only been in this neighborhood for seventeen years."

As Lorraine was walking through the neighborhood, she passed one old house that had been vacant for a good five years. She liked the old two-story house. With renovations, that could be a very luxurious place to live. Actually, it was the most gracious house on the street. The only one with a portico held up by two large wooden columns. Paint was peeling. The paint that was still clinging on was faded and dirty. Some shutters hung on one hinge.

Oh how I wish someone would buy it and restore it. I wish, I wish. What do they say? If you wish hard enough, it will happen. I wish for someone nice to buy this house and restore it.

After a quick shower, with a shower cap protecting her hair, she put on a long white skirt, a green peasant blouse, a wide, red glittery belt, and a fresh red hibiscus in her hair.

"I am pretty," she told her reflection in the long mirror. "I am pretty, I am beautiful, I am desirable. I shall see Alex again and we will dance together. I *am* pretty. You know what, Lori? I believe it myself. My waist could be smaller, but twenty-seven inches isn't bad. Yes, I look nice."

When she went downstairs her father was watching TV. "You look pretty," he said.

Mary gave her usual inspection. "You pass. Have fun."

Frank was dressed in jeans with a western style shirt and leather vest with fringe. "Okay, Sis, you ready to get truckin'?"

"Ready."

"Have a good time kids. Just don't make any noise when you come in."

"We won't, Dad. Good night."

As they walked to the pick-up truck Frank said, "You getting shorter kid?"

"No, why?"

"You always wear high heels to a dance."

"Since we dance on a concrete floor, I want to be kind to my feet, so I wore flats."

"Smart choice. I have my Nikes in the truck just in case the cowboy boots get too uncomfortable. I can go and change."

At the fairgrounds, the big hall was crowded with mostly local young people and competitors from the rodeo who were hoping to pick up a local girl and get lucky. Both Lorraine and Kimberly felt safe being chaperoned by Frank. If any cowboy should get too pushy, all Frank had to do was step in with his six-foot-two-inch frame and tell the boy to get lost.

The three found a space at a table with some acquaintances. The girls took a seat while he went to get something to drink. A beer for himself and two sodas for the girls. Soon a cowboy asked Lorraine to dance, which she did. Then Frank hit the floor with Kimberly and danced a fast two step. After that, the band on the stage played a slow dance. Kimberly put her head on Frank's shoulder as they moved in time with the music.

While struggling on the dance floor with a cowboy who believed he could dance, Lorraine saw Alex enter the hall with Dick and a Mexican girl. Lorraine was able to maneuver her dance partner near to where Alex stood. When she waved to him, he caught her eye. His face lit up with a big grin. She gave him a *come and rescue me* look. Soon the music ended. The cowboy was a gentleman and walked her back to the table. After a smile and thank you, he left and went to join his buddies.

The band had hardly started another song when Alex was at their table, asking Lorraine to dance.

"You look lovely, even prettier than this afternoon. Are you wearing the Mexican colors for me?"

"I would be lying if I said yes. But I did have my clothes laid out before I met you this afternoon. You are a good dancer."

"Gracias, mi amor. You are a graceful dancer yourself. I see your friend here, are you with anyone else?"

"Yes, my brother Frank. After the dance, I would like to introduce you to him."

"I will be happy to meet your brother."

Frank and Kim were at the table when they returned. "Frank, I want you to meet Alex. Alex, this is my brother Frank."

"Nice to meet you Alex. Here let me give you a business card."

"Frank, we are here for fun, not business," Lorraine reprimanded.

"Never know." Frank looked at Alex. "If you're in the market for a car or truck, come see me and I'll see to it that you get a square deal."

Alex looked at the card. "My father's business is looking to buy some new trucks."

"Great, come see me. What business is that?"

"*Lopez Contracting and Reconstruction.* We do mostly water and fire damage work."

"I'm familiar with your firm. So that's your father."

"Yes, I work for him full time. I'm the second man in charge."

Frank gave Lori an approving look. Then the music started a slow melody.

"Excuse me Frank, but would you mind if I have this dance with your sister?"

"Not at all, enjoy. Kimberly, may I have this dance?"

"Always."

The four young people went on the dance floor that was rapidly getting crowded.

Before the evening was over, Alex, along with Dick and his girlfriend Lucina, sat at the table with Frank and the two girls. When they heard the announcement for the last dance, everyone rushed to the floor. What started out as a fast dance was moved into a slow and romantic tune.

Lori and Alex danced with their eyes level with each other. *I'm glad I'm wearing flats, otherwise he would have to look up to me.*

"Lori, I hope this does not end tonight. I really want to see you again."

Oh my God, thank you, he wants to see me again. Little old me. Can this be for real? Can this gorgeous man really be interested in me? Not only is he drop-dead handsome, but he has good manners and is charming. Can this really be for real? "I would like that. I'll write my phone number on the back of the card Frank gave you."

When the dance was over, they lingered on the crowded dance floor. He wrapped his arms around her even tighter and his lips slowly approached hers. She did not move her head away as he came closer until their lips touched and he gave her a kiss that told her volumes about his feelings. She responded as if shouting "Yes, yes, yes."

At home, lying in bed, all she could think of was his face. The music still played in her ears and she felt her body move in time. Dancing with Alexandro, and then the kiss. One kiss, but Lorraine felt her life will never be the same. One glorious wonderful kiss was like electricity surging through her body. She wished he was with her right now, kissing her and doing whatever would follow.

Chapter 2

Lorraine had a hard time concentrating in school the following week. All she could think of was Alex and his beautiful face, his sexy smile showing even white teeth, and his passionate kiss.

Only three more months and I'll graduate. I must keep my grades up. Only three more months and I'll be free, free, free. Free to get a job and earn some money, maybe even get my own apartment. Then I could go out and wear what I want to wear, without having to go through my mother's inspections. Free to wear eye-liner and false lashes if I wish. Life will be wonderful, being free. Come on, time, go ahead and fly by. What do they say? Time flies when you're having fun. Okay time, I'm having fun, now go fly. I can't wait till May gets here and

I'll graduate. Oh, Alex, call me tonight. Call me and tell me sweet nothings. Make a date, I want to see you. We can go dancing, or take a walk in the desert. I don't care what we do, just as long as we're together.

"Lori, can you tell the class what year the Magna Carter was signed?"

"It was signed in 1215."

"Does anyone want to explain the significance of it?"

Some hands were raised.

Why do I need to know what happened in the old days? Fill my head with useless facts. Oh, Alex, come and rescue me.

Then the voice of her teacher swam through her thoughts. "Remember class, those who don't learn from history are forced to repeat it."

It was not until Wednesday after the rodeo that the long awaited phone call came. The phone was in the living room and her father answered it. "It's for you, Lori."

"Hello?"

"Lori, this is Alex."

"Alex, how good to hear from you." She tried to control her excitement. "How are you?"

"Fine, Lori. *Como esta usted?*"

"Muy bien, gracias."

"The reason I called, I was wondering if you would like to attend the music festival on Main Street Saturday night? We could get a bite to eat before the festival."

"That sounds wonderful. I would love to go, but I

have to clear it with my parents first. Hold on." Turning toward her father, she said, "Dad, the young man I met at the rodeo asked me to go to the music festival on Main Street Saturday night. May I go? Frank met him, and he is really nice?"

"Get his number and call him back."

"Oh, Dad," she whispered while holding her hand over the receiver. "Alex, I have to call you back after I speak to my mother. What is your number?" She wrote it down on the pad of paper that was always next to the phone. "You'll hear from me soon. Bye."

Mary Albright entered the room. "Lori, what do you know about that young man?"

"Mom, he is so nice, a good dancer, is working in his father's business, that's about all I know right now."

"You were speaking Spanish. Is he Mexican?"

"Yes, is that a problem? I have lots of Mexican girl-friends and you never seemed to mind."

"Of course not, those are nice girls and I hope they find nice husbands. But you know those Mexican men are hot-blooded and have quick tempers. Dating means shop-ping for a prospective husband."

"Mom, I just met the guy last week. We aren't going to run off and get married next week. We'll be on Main Street, maybe Frank will be there too, and I don't know how many other people I know. What can possibly hap-pen?"

Then Lorne Albright cleared his throat. "Tell you

what, Lori, you tell him you will go, but he will pick you
up at the house and meet your parents."

"Thanks Dad, Mom, you guys are the greatest."

*Whew, now that was a hard job to get past them. I'll
be so glad to be on my own and not have to ask them if I
may take the next breath.* She called him back. "Alex, Yes
I can go out with you Saturday. You may pick me up at
my house and meet my parents."

"I was expecting no less. I wouldn't expect to meet
my princess in secret on the corner. How does five
o'clock sound? Main Street starts at seven. I know this
good restaurant that opened recently."

She told him her address.

"Till Saturday, lovely lady."

Lorraine replaced the receiver, using every effort to
look clam and cool. "He'll be here at five on Saturday.
I'm sure you'll like him."

"We hope so too," said Mary, "but we'd like it more
if you were dating a white boy."

"Now, Mary, don't categorize all Mexicans in the
same box. I work with lots of Mexican men and they are
very decent fellows."

"Yeah, I know, but just pick up the paper and, most
of the time, when there is a crime and they mention the
name, it's Spanish. The most wanted are mostly Hispan-
ics. Are we ready to possibly hitch our wagon to a Mexican family?"

"Mary, they are going on a date. Let's not worry

about something that might never become an issue."

"I'm just thinking ahead in case it becomes an issue."

"I have homework to do," Lorraine said, exasperated. "I'll just go to my room and do it. Good night, Mom and Dad."

"Good night, Lori,"

Her homework was already done, but she used that as an excuse whenever she wanted to get out of a chore or just be left alone. When she got into her room and closed the door, she flopped on her bed, took a pillow, and held it tight to her chest.

"Oh, Alex, Alex, Alex, I love you. There, I said it. Three long, very long days and we'll be together. I want to hold your hands, I want to hear your voice, I want to feel your kiss." She felt a tingling between her legs. "Quiet, girl, maybe you will get some experience soon. I wonder what it feels like to make love."

When Lorraine came down dressed for her date with Alex her mother gave the usual inspection.

"Black jeans pass, but that crop top has to go. First of all, you know how cool it gets at night. Now run upstairs, put on a decent shirt, and take a sweater then come down a few minutes after the young man arrives."

"Yes, Mom." She rushed up the steps. While choosing a chenille sweater she heard a car pull up. Looking out the small dormer window, she saw a red Camero park at the curb. Alex got out and walked toward the house. A knock on the door was answered by her father.

"Good evening, I'm Alexandro Lopez. Is this where Lori lives?"

"You're in the right place, young man. I'm her father and this is—" he said, pointing toward his wife sitting on the couch, "—Mary Albright, her mother."

Alex shook hands with both of them. "Very pleased to meet you."

"That sure is a fancy car you're driving. You get many speeding tickets?"

"That is a 1993 Camero, and no, sir, I don't have any speeding tickets, nor any other tickets."

"That's good. I suppose the payments are pretty substantial on your car," Mr. Albright continued.

"No, sir, it's fully paid for."

"Good for you, young man," he continued. "Where are you working?"

"I'm foreman for Lopez Construction."

"That's good. You hardly look old enough to be a foreman," Mrs. Albright chimed in. "How old are you?"

"I'll be twenty-one next month."

Slowly Lorraine came down the steps. Alexandro looked at her with admiration.

"Hi, Alex, have they been giving you the third degree?"

"Nothing beyond what any good parents would want to know. Mr. and Mrs. Albright, I can assure you, your daughter is safe with me. I'll bring her back the latest after the music festival ends at midnight. If that is agreeable with you?"

"Have a good time," Mr. Albright said.

"You kids enjoy yourselves."

"Thanks, Mom and Dad." She gave her mom a peck on the cheek and proceeded toward the door.

"Don't I get one?" Mr. Albright asked.

Lorraine blew him a kiss. "I love you too, Dad." Then she left quickly.

At the car Alexandro held the door open for her. "Your chariot is at your service, my princess."

Lorraine blushed and got in. "Nice car. Take me away."

"Where would you like to go?"

"Anywhere you say."

"Want to eat Mexican?"

"Love Mexican. Are we going to Mexico?"

"No. How about Geronimo's on Orange Street?"

"Great."

After a short drive, they pulled into the restaurant parking lot and Alexandro moved to get out of the car.

"Alex, please wait, I really need an appetizer."

He looked at her with a question on his face. "We can order one inside."

"Not that kind, just a little kiss would be good."

He went around to the passenger door, opened it, and gave her his hand. When she stood, he took her in his arms and kissed her on the mouth. After the first kiss, he kissed her again with his tongue moving in her mouth.

Lorraine opened her eyes wide. She did not know such a kiss existed. *I just have to read some romance novels.* Then another car pulled into the parking lot. Alex took Lori's hand and led her into the restaurant.

Chapter 3

The next few weeks, Lorraine checked out romance novels from the library. Evenings during the week, she went to her room early and read in bed. She devoured the love scenes and dreamt of herself in one. Saturdays she went on dates with Alex, Sundays she went to church for the early mass. She asked Alex what his religion was, and was delighted when he told her he was a Catholic.

"Which church you go to, Alex?"

"St. Francis of Assisi."

"I go there too, wonder why I've never seen you."

"I usually go to Spanish mass. My mother likes it and I take her."

"Doesn't your mother drive?"

"Yes, she drives."

"My Spanish is pretty good. Maybe I could meet you at mass there next Sunday?"

"That is really my alone time with my mother. I like to keep it that way."

I would think he would want me to meet his mother. Maybe to the Mexicans, when a boy brings a girl home to meet his mother, they are as good as engaged. I don't want to be pushy, but I wish he would want me to meet his family. His birthday is coming up soon. I wonder what I could give him as a present. I wonder if there will be a party he'll invite me to."

Alexandro's twenty-first birthday fell on a Sunday. Lorraine had a date with him Saturday night for dinner and a movie. They both enjoyed *Forrest Gump*. After the movie, they drove toward the foothills and parked at the end of a road. They sat in the front seat of the car and looked at the three-quarter moon through the windshield. He leaned over and took her in his arms to kiss her.

"Ouch," he said, "the steering wheel is poking me and the stick shift is in the way. I have a blanket in the trunk. Let's just sit on that and look at the moon."

"I have a birthday present for you. May I give it to you now?"

"Sure, can I open it?"

"If you want, or maybe you'll want to open it tomorrow. Aren't you having a party?"

"I meant to tell you, my family is taking me to San

Luis, Mexico, for a family party. We have quite a few relatives over there, and they are putting on a fiesta in my honor."

"That sounds like fun. Wish I could be there."

"I would take you, but then my family would think we are ready to get married. You are not even out of high school yet."

"Are you saying I'm too young for you?"

"No, no, I'm only three years older than you—well, actually three and a half. My parents have seven years between them."

"And my father is eight years older than my mother."

"I'm just not ready to get married at this time, otherwise I would take you. Now where is that present?"

While Alexandro went to the trunk to retrieve the blanket, she reached under the seat, brought out a small package, and gave it to him.

"Here it is, and have a very happy birthday."

"Thank you." He opened it. "CDs of my favorite artists. Thank you, so much. You want a beer?"

"I never drink beer. My mother would kill me."

"Forbidden fruit is all the sweeter. I dare you to defy your mother."

"Then let me have a beer. It's about time I have something worthwhile for confession."

They sat by the light of the moon, drinking beer. Lorraine did not like the taste of it, but knowing she was being naughty made it fun. Besides, Alex liked his beer and

seemed pleased that she drank with him. After she finished the first can, Alex gave her another one and some
munchies to go with it. Then he kissed her passionately
on the lips while his hands groped her breasts for the first
time.

"Sweet princess, you have such a beautiful body.
Please let me see it and feel it."

"Oh, Alex, promise you won't go all the way. I want
to save myself for my husband."

"I'm sure your mother instilled that in you. Good for
her. I believe that is what you should do, just let me have
a peek at what I would get if I become your husband."

She didn't fight him as he lifted her shirt above her
breasts. She did not resist as his tongue tickled her nipples. She was almost in a dream as his hands groped lower and lower, playing with her pubic hair. She helped him
take off her jeans.

"Now, you promised, you won't go all the way. Just
a look and a little feel."

"Oh sweetheart, you are the prettiest sight I have ever seen. Let me look at you some more, let me feel and
kiss every inch of your gorgeous body."

She closed her eyes and enjoyed the moment. She
was unaware that he had removed his pants, so skillfully
did he play with her. Then it happened.

She knew it was a mistake the moment he entered
her. There was the pain. All the romance novels she had
read only described the feelings of passion and bliss.

None mentioned how painful it was the first time. She called for him to stop, but he kept going, deeper and deeper, almost with a vengeance. Suddenly all the soft pleasant feelings felt like torture. It seemed forever that he was bouncing on her until he finally reached a climax. He cried out with pleasure, then rolled off her, looking at his bloody penis.

He looked at it with an evil grin. Like a warrior that had just scaled the castle wall and was ready to claim his spoils. He looked down at her lying naked on a blanket in the desert.

"I know the first time hurts, but it gets better."

"I'm sure you do. I suppose I am not the first virgin you have put your rod into."

"Oh, honey, you were great. You'll make some guy a good wife."

"Some guy? What about all the love you professed for me? You indicated that we might have a future together. Don't you love me anymore or were you just lying?"

"No, no, I didn't lie. I do love you." He took her in his arms. "Honey, you're getting cold. You better put your clothes back on. It's getting late. I better take you home."

"Oh, Alex, hold me, make the pain go away. It still hurts and I feel so dirty. You promised you wouldn't go all the way."

"I know, I just got carried away, and when you didn't

stop me, I just thought it was good with you. I'll make it up to you, I promise."

"There is no way you can make it up to me."

"I'll send you a big bouquet of flowers on Monday."

"Yeah, how would I explain that to my parents?"

"Lori, I love you, and that is the truth. Now let's go home."

At the door, he gave her a quick good night kiss and promised to call her when he got back from Mexico if it wasn't too late. Otherwise, he'd call her Monday evening. Softly she went into the house and went upstairs. Since running a shower might wake up her parents who were sleeping on the first floor, she just washed herself. She was amazed how much blood there was. She washed her panties in the sink. She did not want her mother to find bloody pants in the middle of her month. Then she put a feminine napkin in her pants and went to bed. She lay there a long time with her vagina hurting. She felt soiled and wondered if romance was worth the price.

Chapter 4

Getting ready for graduation and starting a job search kept Lorraine busy for the next few weeks. Once a week she did have a date with Alex. They would either go to a dance or go for a drive or take long walks in the desert. One day, while they were walking in her neighborhood, they passed the two-story house in need of renovation.

"I like that house," Alexandro said. "Let's walk around it, I want to see it."

"I like that house, too. I have been wishing for someone to buy it and fix it up."

"I think it would be a good investment. Tomorrow, I'll look up who the owner is and get in contact if I can. Maybe we can deal."

Lori heard the excitement in his voice. Suddenly she fell in love with him all over. It would be so much fun helping him work on this lovely old house. "Alex?"

"What dear?"

"You said that making love would feel better after a while. You willing to try again?"

"Any time you want to."

"I want to."

"In the desert?" he asked.

"In the desert. When?"

"Why not now?"

Off they went in his red sports car and made love in the desert in the afternoon.

One afternoon, while putting away clean underwear in her dresser, Lori came across a box of sanitary napkins.

"Oh my God, it can't be. I haven't had a period for six weeks. Oh holy Jesus and Mother Mary, don't tell me I'm pregnant."

The next time she went out with her friend Kimberly, she asked her to stop a drug store away from her neighborhood. There she bought a pregnancy test kit. She could not wait to get home and try it. The news shocked her.

How could I be? I've only done it twice. That must have happened the very first time. Wow, I'm fertile. Now what will I do? Mom and Dad will kill me. I have to speak with Alex.

She called him while he was working. He seemed annoyed receiving a phone call while on the job.

"Alex, it is very important, but I need to see you. Can we get together tonight?"

"I won't get off until at least six PM. After I clean up, I'll come over and we can go to the park."

"Sounds good, see you then."

While they were walking silently in the park, Alex finally asked, "What's so important that you need to see me about right away?"

"Alex, I missed two periods and the pregnancy test showed positive."

"Wow, that's a mouthful in a few words. What do you plan of doing about it?"

"What do you mean, what do I plan in doing about it? This baby is yours too. The last thing in the world I want to be is a single mother. Remember, I'm still under eighteen and legally that is statutory rape. You could be going to jail."

"So my choice is either jail or getting married. Pick the worse of the two."

If he says he'd rather go to jail, I'll die.

"Okay, sweetheart, Let us have a wedding." He hugged her and gave her a kiss on the lips.

"Oh, Alex, you make me the happiest girl in the world. Now when will I meet your family?"

"Tell you what. We'll tell your family tonight, and then next weekend we'll have a fiesta and celebrate our

engagement. How would you like to have a June wedding?"

"Great, I should still have a waistline then."

The Albrights were sitting in the living room watching the local news on television when the two young people entered.

"Hello, Alex," Mrs. Albright said brushing a red, out-
of-the-bottle strand of hair off her forehead. "What brings
you here on a Wednesday?"

"Mr. and Mrs. Albright, I have come to ask both of
you a serious question."

Lorne shut off the TV with his remote. "Oh, oh. Now
Alex, what is it you want to know?"

"I have come to ask you for Lori's hand in marriage."

"Marriage!" Mary shouted in a high-pitched voice
while getting to her feet. "You kids hardly know each
other and you both are so young."

"We love each other," said Alex.

"I hope you are planning on a long engagement," Mr.
Albright commented.

"No, Mom and Dad, we would really like a June
wedding."

"Next year in June, or maybe the year after that,"
Mary Albright said hopefully.

"No, we were thinking of this coming June," Alex
said.

"What makes you want to rush this?" Mrs. Albright

asked, looking at her daughter very intensely. "You're not pregnant—or are you?"

Lorraine lowered her head in shame. "Yes I am," she whispered.

"Alexandro, how could you do this to our daughter?" Mary shouted. "Lori, I raised you to be a decent girl and to save yourself until you are married."

"I'm sorry, Mom and Dad," Lorraine cried with big tears running down her cheeks.

Alex put a protective arm on her shoulder and pulled her into his embrace. "I love Lori and I'll be a good husband and father. I hope we have your blessings."

"Son," Lorne said, "we have to accept the situation as it is. I was hoping for our daughter to graduate from high school and work for a while before she gets into being a wife and mother. But since that is not going to happen, we'll just have to accept facts and make the best of it. Personally, you have my blessings, what do you say, Mary?"

"What can I say since you said it all? That does not give us much time to prepare for a wedding. We have not even met any of your family yet. When can that happen?"

"I'll tell the good news to my folks tonight. I'm sure they'll make an engagement party this coming Saturday and you will get to meet everybody then. I'll call you in a day or two to tell you the time and address."

Lorne rose from the sofa and shook the boy's hand. "Welcome to the family, Alex."

"Thank you, sir."

"Welcome, son-in-law," Mary said, giving him a hug. Then she hugged her daughter. "Lorne, can you imagine us being grandparents? Aren't we too young to be grandparents?"

"We aren't that young at past forty. The youngest grandmother I ever met was only thirty-two."

"Do I look like a grandmother?"

"No dear, you still look like my young girlfriend."

Mary chuckled and gave him a loving look. "I just hope you kids will be as happy with each other as we are."

"We intend to be, won't we, Alex?"

"I'll do everything in my power to make you happy," Alex said, giving her a kiss on the cheek. "I better be getting home now. My mother goes to bed early and we have a lot to talk about."

"We understand," Mary said. "Goodbye, see you soon."

"Have you met any of his relatives?" Mr. Albright asked after Alex left.

"No, not yet."

"I wish you had," he said with a worried look.

Chapter 5

Saturday dawned a bright clear typical desert day. The crisp morning air gave way to a comfortably warm day. The party was to start at two in the afternoon. Lorraine dressed in a white Mexican cotton dress with a full handkerchief hem skirt embroidered with multicolored flowers. Again her hair was decorated with a red hibiscus. The Lopez house was located in an affluent part of Yuma. The white two-story house had a large family room open to the kitchen, a formal dining room with a tray ceiling and a large crystal chandelier. The formal living room had white upholstered furniture accented with carved wood. French doors lead out to the patio containing numerous tables with chairs. A kidney shaped swimming pool sparkled with crystal-clear water.

"Wow," was all Mary Albright managed to say while they stood in the foyer. "I never expected Mexicans to live like this."

"You have to stop thinking of them as Mexicans. They are Americans just like us," Lorne whispered into Mary's ear.

Lorraine stood next to her parents, waiting for Alexandro to escort them in.

"Ah, there you are, my sweet," he said, approaching them and reaching both hands out to Lorraine. "Welcome to my home, Mr. and Mrs. Albright. Come and meet everyone." He led them toward a woman supervising the caterers.

A slim, very attractive woman with long black hair in large curls greeted them with a big smile. "So, I finally get to meet my new daughter. I don't know what's wrong with Alex that he didn't bring you around a lot sooner, child, welcome," she said, giving Lorraine a lengthy hug. "And so nice to meet you too, Mr. and Mrs. Albright."

"Please call us Lorne and Mary," said Mary, giving Mrs. Lopez a hug.

"And you can call me Elena. Here comes my husband Juan."

He too greeted everyone warmly.

"I'm having everyone wearing a name tag with their names and relationship to Alex," Elena said. "That should make it easy for you to find your way around these fifty or so relatives that are here. Please make a name-tag for yourselves, too. I understand your son and some friends of yours are coming too."

"Yes, Frank gets off at five, and he'll bring one of Lori's friends."

"Good, the more the merrier, I always say. We'll be serving lunch soon, and the bar is on the other side of the pool, just meet everybody and enjoy."

They could hear music playing from outside.

"Good, the mariachis have started. You like to dance? Feel free to," Elena said, turning back to the caterer who had just dropped a big lid making a loud clang on the tile floor.

Outside, people were dancing or just sitting around talking. Others were in the pool, including about ten children. When they got too wild and ran near the pool, a young man, especially hired to act as lifeguard, reprimanded them and calmed them down. All of the Lopez clan was very friendly and made the Albrights feel welcome. Shortly after Frank and Kimberly arrived there was a formal ceremony.

Juan Lopez stood on an elevated platform that had been built as a bandstand. He raised his arms and asked for everyone's attention. In a clear loud voice he announced that everyone was here for his son Alexandro and his bride to be, Lori. "Come up here you two, so everyone can see."

Alexandro led Lorraine up to the bandstand while everyone clapped and cheered. Then he fell to one knee and, taking Lorraine's hand, he asked her to be his wife. When she said yes, he took a ring out of his pocket and put it on her finger. It was a solitaire with a round one carat diamond. Lorraine raised him up and gave him a big hug.

"Oh darling, thank you. I am so happy. I promise I will be a good wife to you." Then she whispered, "And I would never have accused you of rape."

They kissed while everyone cheered and clapped.

"When will the wedding be?" An elderly aunt of his asked Lorraine.

"Next week I graduate from high school, then we were thinking on Saturday, June twenty-fourth to get married."

"Oh, so soon?" And the aunt lowered her gaze to Lorraine's waist line.

"It will be at St Francis church with a small reception in the church hall."

"Nothing is small with the Lopez clan. You better be prepared for several hundred people."

"Thanks for the warning. I'll discuss it with my mom."

Juan came up and asked Lorraine to dance. Alexandro was dancing with Mary and Lorne was spinning Elena around, making her red skirt flare, showing off her long legs.

It was well after midnight before the Albrights got home.

"Now those people know how to party," Mary said with a big grin. "Lorne, we need to practice dancing to keep up with them. Come, Lorne, let's go to bed and exercise."

Lorraine smiled as she went up the steps. *There is some life in the old folks yet.*

Chapter 6

Graduation passed in a blur. It was the upcoming wedding that took all of Lorraine's attention. Mr. Albright was a foreman in a produce warehouse. He made a decent living for the family, but compared to the Lopezes they could not hold a candle.

The three Albrights sat in the living room of their small house, discussing the upcoming wedding.

"Lorne, we'll just allow a $5,000 budget for the wedding, and I'm sure we can do it. I'll take Lori to that big discount bridal shop in Phoenix to get her dress. As far as food for the reception, there are enough caterers in Yuma for me to negotiate with."

"The key word is negotiate, and that, my dear, is your forte," Lorne said cheerfully. "We're fortunate to get the church hall for just a donation since our family has been members since the beginning. How many people should we plan for?"

"The latest estimate I got was 150, but that could go up," Mary said. "What do you think, Lori?"

"Huh, oh yes, 150 or 160 should do it," Lori answered coming out of the daydream of the house up the street which Alex had bought and was busy having his crew renovate. They were working on it mostly in the evenings and on weekends, many donating their time as a wedding present to their boss. Most of them considered him not only a boss but also a friend.

After the new windows were installed, the outside was painted a grayish blue with white trim. Now the crew was working on the inside, installing the jet bathtub Lori wished for, and tiling the bathroom. Alex had promised her that the house would be finished for them to move into right after the wedding.

She knew that, from here on, her life would only be wonderful. In addition to one bridal magazine, there were several books and magazines of home decoration laying on the living room coffee table.

"We'll miss having you live here, Lori," Lorne said, "but thank God you will be close."

Maybe too close for comfort, Lori thought. *But on the other hand, it will be a convenient place to drop off the baby when we want to go out.* She rubbed her belly, *right Junior? How terrible of me, I haven't even felt a kick yet and here I'm looking for a baby sitter. You just keep right on sleeping, sweet child.*

When Lorraine put on her white wedding dress, she could feel the first kick. "Oh sweet baby, you too are jumping for joy. Hallelujah, praise the Lord."

A family friend was the official photographer and he caught the moment Mary put the bridal veil on Lorraine.

"White veils are a sign of virginity. You disappointed me, my daughter," she said with tears in her eyes.

"Yes, Mother, I'm sorry. Now please don't smear your make-up."

Downstairs in the living room, her three bridesmaids, dressed in three shades of green, were waiting with Mr. Albright who looked handsome in his rented black tuxedo with green cummerbund. When Lorraine came down the steps with the bannister squeezing her full skirt, they gave sighs of approval. "You look beautiful, my girl." said her father. "He is one lucky man to get you."

"Yes, you are lovely," Kimberly said, "want to trade? I wish it was me getting married today. And to move into that beautiful house up the street, you are so lucky. I wish you tons of happiness."

"Thank you, and thank you for being here for me today."

"Frank, you ready to go?" Mary called upstairs.

"Almost, I'm having trouble tying my tie."

"Come on downstairs and I'll help you," called Lorne.

Since Frank was not in the wedding party, he was dressed in dark gray slacks and a blue blazer. Kimberly's face lit up when he came down the steps. Then everyone got into the white stretch limousine waiting at the curb.

"Come, my beautiful two ladies," said Lorne, "time to go to church and get a son."

Lorraine went through the rest of the day as if in a dream. She knew she was the center of attention, but somehow it seemed to her she was watching a movie. The church hall was big enough for everyone, and the Lopez clan had decorated the hall and provided a mariachi band. There was a three tier wedding cake, the first dance of the newlyweds, and the dance with both fathers. Then any one could buy a dance with the bride or groom. That was to be their honeymoon money. Only later did Lorraine learn that it not only paid for the honeymoon in San Diego, but there was enough to buy a new couch for the living room. *This is supposed to be the happiest day of my life, but I feel that I'm not even here. I'll come back to earth eventually. I just hope the fall will not be a hard landing. Oh sweet Jesus, please bless us always.*

After the reception in church, the young couple, still dressed in their wedding attire, drove in the red Camaro over the mountains to the Hotel del Coronado in San Diego. It was still daylight as they arrived in the large, dark wood lobby. Everyone who saw them waved and shouted greeting of good luck and blessings as they were escorted to their room overlooking the ocean. When the porter closed the door from the outside, Alexandro took Lori in his arms.

"Privacy at last. Now it is totally legal and decent for us to make love."

And they did.

Chapter 7

In the next few months, Lorraine was totally emerged in being a wife and looking forward to becoming a mother. Her cooking was limited, but some dishes she did really well. When the pork chops she served were moist and tender, Alexandro would praise her. When something did not turn our as well as expected, he would still eat it without making a face.

She had gotten a learner's permit while still in school and when she felt ready to take a driving test, Kimberly let her do it in her little Honda. That evening she was excited to show Alex her license.

"Look, Alex, I can drive now. How do you like the picture on my license?"

"Not bad. Now does that mean you want a car?"

"Well, a car would come in handy, especially when we have the baby. I'll need to take it to the doctor and all that. Do you think we can afford for me to get a little used car?"

"Tell you what. Tell your brother, Frank, you need a car that costs no more than $5,000."

"Oh, Alex, you are the best husband a girl could ever have. Thank you, thank you, thank you," she said, walking around the back of him and showering his hair and face with kisses.

"You ready for bed?"

"I was hoping you would help me hang curtains, but okay, we can do that first."

"We might as well enjoy our alone time while we still have it," he said, leading her into the bedroom.

She wondered if he would ever get enough sex. *What about when the baby comes and I'm out of commission for a few weeks? Will he look for sex somewhere else?*

෬෩෬

"What are you doing for Thanksgiving?" Mary asked her daughter as they were taking a leisurely walk in the neighborhood.

"I was thinking of hosting a dinner at my house. Invite you and Dad and Madre y Padre Lopez and, of course, Frank and his girlfriend Kimberly. What do you think, Mom, do you think I can handle it?"

"Do you believe you can handle having a dinner party for eight people?"

"Yeah, I think I can. Of course, the cooking won't be as good as yours."

"Honey, you keep underestimating yourself. If you decide to do it, I'm sure it will be delicious. If you want, I can bring some pies."

"That would be great. We better get back home, I have to pee again. I think this kid is playing football with my bladder."

"The joys of pregnancy. Just think, it won't be much longer and we'll have another member in the family. I bet your father will just be wrapped around the baby's little finger."

"I think he is almost more excited about me having a baby than I am."

"Oh, why do you say that?"

"Sometimes I feel excited and other times the thought simply scares me. Will I be able to take the pain of childbirth?"

"Of course you can. If natural birth gets too overwhelming, the doctor can relieve your pain. Are you still doing your exercises?"

"Yes, every day."

"You'll do fine."

"I'm worried that Alex might not be able to stand watching the delivery. He said he faints at the sight of blood."

"Oh, did he faint when you two did it for the first time?"

"No he did not." She remembered his evil grin when he saw the blood on his penis. Even shone a flashlight on it so he could see it better. Lorraine shuddered. "Here we are. Come in so we can discuss Thanksgiving dinner some more after I go to the bathroom."

☙❧❧

When the big day came, Lorraine grew both excited and nervous about her first diner party.

The aroma of cooking permeated throughout the house, giving it a festive mood.

"That is what this house needs, a real dinner party," Alex said as he pulled the fifteen pound turkey out of the oven. "Our guests should be arriving any minute now."

A car parked at the curb and Mr. and Mrs. Lopez emerged, carrying several bottles of wine. At the same time, the Albrights came walking up the street, each one carrying a pie. Soon Frank and Kimberly arrived in his pick-up truck. Warm greetings with lots of hugs were exchanged all around. Everyone complemented Lorraine and Alexandro on the beautiful job they had done with the dinner.

"It is nice to see you using the Limoges china you got as a wedding present," said Elena Lopez.

"Of course, one uses the present given by the best mother-in-law a girl could have."

"She's not the only one lucky in that department," Alex said. "I have the best mother and father-in-law a man could have."

Everyone laughed.

"I'll drink to that," said Lorne, raising his glass.

"And I want to propose a toast to our children and the baby soon to come," said Juan Lopez, raising his glass. "May they have a long and happy life together, and may all their troubles be little ones."

"Ooh," Lori said, "that little one just answered your toast with a resounding kick." Then she drank her white grape juice out of the crystal wine glass. "Thank you for all your love and support."

At the conclusion of dinner Frank tapped his wine glass for everyone's attention.

"Kimberly and I have something to announce too," he said.

"What is that?" Asked Mary.

"This morning I asked Kimberly to marry me."

"And?" asked Mary.

"And she said yes."

"Who-ho," Mary shouted with delight as she rose to hug her son and Kimberly.

"Congratulations, best wishes and all good things," said Lorne.

There was another hug-fest, lasting a good ten

minutes. While everyone was up and talking excitedly about an upcoming wedding, Lorraine sat on the sofa and was very quiet. After a while Mary asked,

"Lori, are you okay?"

"Yes, Mom, but I think I might be in labor."

"Now?" Alex asked, concerned. "I thought we had another two weeks?"

"I did too."

"It might be false labor," Elena said. "I had false labor several times with my pregnancy. Do you have contractions? Let us know when you get one and we'll time it."

"I have one right now."

"Does it hurt?" Alex asked.

"No, it doesn't hurt yet, but I can feel my muscles working. There, it's over."

"Let us know if you get another one," Mary demanded.

"Well, don't just stand around staring at me. Go and have some of Mom's pie."

They all went back to the dining room and had pie with either ice cream or whipped cream, while Lori sat on the couch, waiting for the next contraction.

"I feel one," she shouted into the dining room.

"That's only five minutes," Lorne announced, alarmed.

"We better call the doctor and get ready to go to the hospital," Mary added.

"I can't leave now, I have to clean up after dinner," Lorraine complained.

"Don't worry about it," Kimberly interjected, "Frank and I will clean up for you, won't we, Frank? You really did do a terrific job with dinner."

"That's right, Sis, don't worry, we'll clean everything up."

Mary hung up the phone. "The doctor said for you to come to the hospital and he'll check you there to see if it's real labor. What a way to end a Thanksgiving party. Who all is going?"

"We are," answered the Lopezes.

"Mary and I are going, too. Now, you two kids," Lorne said, looking at Frank and Kimberly, "stay here and take care of everything."

"Yes, Dad, and happy pushing, you two."

Chapter 8

Two days later, the young Lopez couple came home with a little pink bundle. In a matter of minutes, the house was filled with relatives and neighbors eager to see the little girl.

"Oh, what a beautiful baby, look how much dark hair she has. What is her name?" was accompanied with many sounds of praises.

Elena held the baby for all to see but not touch. "Her name is Rachel," she exclaimed proudly. "This is my first grandchild,"

"One would never believe you are a grandmother," commented some neighbors.

"This is my first grandchild too," Mary chimed in, hoping for the same compliment.

"Congratulations," and "enjoy your grand-baby," were the comments she got.

"Lori needs her rest," Alex said, "and it's almost nursing time."

"We get the hint," said one neighbor. "I baked a cake. May I bring some of it over later?"

"That would be lovely," Lorraine exclaimed. "Thank you all for coming and welcoming us home. Good-bye."

As soon as the neighbors left the house the baby let out a loud cry.

"She must be hungry," Mary said. "Now you better get her on a schedule right away and only feed her when it's time."

"I fed my baby on demand," Elena disagreed. "Why hear the cry of a hungry baby when one can feed it that moment?"

"If you don't want to spoil the child right off the bat," Mary said, looking at Lorraine, "you will adhere to a strict schedule."

"You can't spoil a tiny little baby like that. I say, feed her when she's hungry," Elena argued, raising her voice.

"Ladies, ladies, now don't get into a fight over this," Alexandro interjected. "Lori will develop her own schedule for the baby."

"Yes, Mom and Madre, I really would like to get some rest now. Thanks for visiting, but I want to go to bed and nurse the baby."

She proceeded to walk up the steps, while Alex carried the baby up-stairs. The two grandmothers left the house, debating the raising of a child.

"In the future," Alex said, "we'll try not to have them visit at the same time."

"And I will feed the baby on demand."

While Lorraine was lying on her side, nursing the baby, she fell asleep. When Alex went to put her in the crib next to the bed, he felt her diaper. Since it was wet he proceeded to change it. Upon removal of the wet diaper he looked at the bottom of his daughter with great fascination. He stood there staring at it. Lori woke up and saw him staring at the baby's bare bottom. She peeked at him through closed eyelids. Soon Alex was rubbing at the crotch of his pants. When the baby cried, he quickly continued with the diapering.

Oh God, no, I hope he isn't a pervert. I have to keep an eye on him.

෴

Before Lorraine went for her six week check-up, there was no sex. Alex put in some long days at work then, sometimes not coming home until ten at night. Lori wondered about his faithfulness, but said nothing. He always called her on his cell phone and told her if he would be late and for her not to save supper. Then finally she had the six-week examination. Mary watched the baby while she went to the doctor. Before she picked up Rachel from the parent's house, she went home to change her clothes and was surprised by Alex being home and giving her a big bouquet of red roses.

"Flowers for my beautiful lady. What did the doctor say?"

"He gave us the green light."

"Yippee, can you hear my engine is revved up and ready to roar?"

"What are you waiting for?"

They both rushed up to the bedroom.

A few months later Lorraine was pregnant again. Just thirteen months later she delivered a boy they named Jaime, but called him Jimmy. Just a little more than a year later, Lori was again in the delivery room giving birth to another girl they named Maria. While still in the labor room she had the opportunity to have a private talk with her obstetrician.

"Doctor, this is getting old. You know I'm Catholic and I'm just to pump out kids as they come, but I can't take it. I find myself getting short tempered more and more. Is there anything you can do to stop this production?"

"Of course, there are several ways—"

"But can you do it so my husband doesn't know?"

"We can discuss it when you come for your post-natal check-up. Here comes your husband now."

"Hi, sweetheart, I came as quickly as I could get away from the job. How are you feeling?"

"It hurts like hell. Alex, promise me you'll have the next one, I'm tired of this."

"Of course, you are," he said condescendingly, "I promise to have the next baby for you."

"*Liar*." She laughed then twisted her face into a grimace.

∽∾∽

Two weeks after the birth, Lori fell into a deep depression. By now she had figured out that it was only when she was sexually out of commission that Alex would have to work overtime. She wondered who or how many were her substitute. Sometimes she felt a rage, then a few minutes later she did not care. She felt she was nothing but a milk-cow surrounded by shitty diapers. Three babies in diapers was more than she was willing to handle.

Maria was five weeks old when Alex changed her diaper. Two year old Rachel was watching as her father stared at the baby's bare bottom. Soon he unzipped his jeans and played with himself. Just then Lori silently entered the room.

At first she just stood there in shock, then she went into a rage.

"You pervert, what the hell do you think you are doing? How dare you expose yourself in front of your daughter?" She grabbed Rachel and put her into the playroom where her brother was sitting on the floor.

"Play nice with Jimmy now," she said, closing the door as she left.

Returning to the bedroom, she took the now diapered baby and put her into the crib. Alex was still standing there. "How dare you? Don't ever expose yourself."

"It's all your fault. I wouldn't be so horny if you gave me oral sex."

"That's right, blame me for everything. It's all my fault, you oversexed pervert. Why don't you get a vasectomy so I don't get pregnant all the time?"

"You know that would be a sin."

"Sin, sin, everything is a sin. I bet my bottom dollar that you have committed adultery since we've been married. I kept a blind eye, but I'm tired of it." Her voice became louder.

"Shh, you don't want the neighbors to hear us. You better cool off. Until you do, I'm going out."

He ran down the stairs and out the front door. She heard his car start in the driveway and take off down the street. Lorraine threw herself on the bed and cried.

She did not know how long she lay there crying until Rachel came into the room. "Mommy, I'm hungry."

When Alex returned late at night and crawled into the queen sized bed, Lorraine could smell the alcohol. She got up, went into the children's room, and slept on the day bed.

The next day, when she got up, he was already gone.

A few days later, she had the doctor put in an IUD.

"This device is ninety-eight per cent effective," the doctor reassured her.

"What are the side effects?"

"You might have a heavier than normal period, but there is medicine for that."

The doctor told her that sex would most likely be more fun not having to worry about getting pregnant, but that was not the case. Lorraine felt that Alex went through the motions, sometimes even giving her a nice gift. Not only did he remember Mother's Day and Valentine, but also she got little surprises for the children's birthdays.

"Alex is the most thoughtful and loving husband," her mother said. "You should be so grateful and not constantly be blue."

"I know, Mom, I just can't seem to shake the postpartum depression."

"Maybe you should see a counselor. You have so much to be thankful for, three beautiful, healthy children, a lovely home, your own car, nice in-laws. What more could you ask for?"

"I know, Mom."

"I tell you what. Bring all three kids to my house Saturday afternoon, and be alone with Alex for a while. Make love with him without having to worry about a baby starting to cry."

"Thanks, Mom, you're right. It seems like every time

we are intimate, one of the babies starts crying. It sure breaks the mood."

Chapter 9

Alex arrived that Saturday afternoon from work to a quiet house and romantic music. The aroma of roast beef made his mouth water. Lorraine wore a pretty blue dress, covered with an apron. The dining room table was set with good china, candles, and champagne glasses.

"This looks like a dinner party table set for two."

"It is a dinner party for us two."

"Did I miss a special occasion?"

"No dear, you made it in time for the special occasion. The kids are with my parents and we are alone this evening." She took the telephone off the hook and asked him to shut off the cell phone.

After dinner, they sat in the living room in front of

the fireplace and enjoyed some more champagne. Soon the two were carried away, like they had not been for a long time. Suddenly all responsibility and depression were forgotten and the two were lost in their passion for each other.

"Oh, Alex, that was wonderful, you make me feel good."

"Now I want something for you to make me feel good." His body language told her he wanted oral sex.

"No, Alex, I can't. Please don't demand that."

He slapped her hard on the face. "Damn it, you are my wife. You are to do what I tell you."

"Alex, please, anything but that."

"Anything, you say. Then that you shall get." He removed the leather belt from his jeans and beat her across her naked buttocks.

"Ow, you're hurting me, stop it." She put her fingers where she was struck and felt welts rising.

"You said anything, either that or what I asked for."

"Okay, stop, I will do it."

"And you better not bite."

After they finished Alex took her gently in his arms and kissed her all over her body.

"Thank you, sweetheart, you are the greatest."

"I don't like getting beaten."

"I'm sorry, that won't ever happen again. You know I love you. You are the best little wife a man could wish for. Forgive me, I was a bad boy."

"I forgive you, but don't ever let that happen again."

"But you will do oral sex from now on, won't you?"

"Will you do it to me?"

"What? You expect me to do that?"

"A tit for a tat."

"What the hell does that mean?"

"What's good for the goose is good for the gander."

"Okay, next time we are alone, I'll do it to you."

"Why not right now?"

"I've had enough sex for today. We better get the baby." He squeezed her breasts. "Your breasts are filling up."

"Ow, that hurts."

⌘

Mary opened the door expectantly. "Good, you are here. I tried giving Maria the bottle, but she did not want any part of it. She's been fussy for over an hour. The other two are sleeping soundly. You might as well leave them here for the night."

"Thank you Mom, we'll get them in the morning."

"You kids have a good evening?" Lorne asked.

"Great Dad, thank you again for taking them for a few hours. Good night."

They took the baby, got in the mini-van, and drove around the corner to their house. Then Lori proceeded to nurse the baby.

"What a beautiful sight, seeing mother and child connect like that. I just have to take a picture."

"Alex, please don't. I'm afraid you'll put it on social media."

"No, I won't."

"You said that too when you put on the picture of me right after delivery and I looked like crap."

"You never look like crap, my beautiful princess."

"Oh, Alex," He snapped a picture. "Now please, no social media with this picture, promise."

"I promise." After the baby was satisfied and Lorraine changed her diaper, they all turned in for the night. To everyone's surprise, the baby slept all night, too. "Maybe it's the champagne I drank last night that made the baby sleep all night. I don't remember when I had a full eight hours last."

"Hmm, maybe you should take up drinking."

"Yeah, right, you want me to become a lush?"

"No, not a lush, just my little whore."

"Don't you even think of me as a whore. I am your wife and the mother of your three children."

"You are right, dear, and soon there will be even more children."

"How many children do you want, Alex? We never discussed that before we got married."

"An even dozen would not be too many as far as I'm concerned."

"Alex, I feel sometimes overwhelmed with three

children. I hope it will be a while before the next one comes."

"You are beautiful when you are pregnant. I want you like that all the time."

"Where does that idea come from? Your mother stopped after one, and she is happy with her family."

"Well then, let's try for number four right now."

"Alex, not now, it's time to get ready for church."

"Great idea, we'll go to church, drop the kids off at the nursery, go out into the parking lot, and do it in the mini-van."

"Alex, do you ever get enough?"

"Hey, I'm young and virile. Remember there were a few weeks with no action between us."

"I can't help but wonder who you had action with," she mused. "Aren't we supposed to meet your mother and father at church?"

"Yeah, I forgot. We'll just have to wait till the kids take a nap then."

"Oh, Alex, I think you're hopeless. Now let's go to church."

೧೦೧

A few months later, while Lori was busy with the laundry, Alex was upstairs changing the baby's diaper. Again he looked at the girl's bare bottom, reached into his pants, and pulled it out. He stood there masturbating while staring at the baby. Just then, Lori came up the carpeted stairs and entered the room.

"You pig, you damn pig, what the hell do you think you are doing?"

"I'm not hurting anyone."

"Next thing, you will start having sex with the girls. I think you should be the one seeing a counselor, not me. Oh my God and holy Jesus, what am I going to do?"

What is wrong with that man? Now I'm afraid to leave him alone with the kids while I take a bath. Holy Mary, mother of God help me. Don't let anything bad happen to my precious babies.

"I was just checking to see if my semen looks healthy. It's been close to a year since Maria was born. I was wondering why you're not pregnant."

"There is nothing wrong. My body is just taking a rest."

"Well, we have to wake it up."

"It's as awake as it's going to get with all the chores around here. You leave the house and go to work. When you come home you are done for the day. My work goes on around the clock."

"I know what you need. We'll get a cleaning lady to come in. Do you think once a week will be enough?"

"Once a week will be great, twice a week even better. But I get to hire her."

"Okay, you do that. Just put an ad in the paper."

A few days later, Lorraine hired a middle-aged black

woman to do housework. When the woman came, Lori would take the children and leave the house. After a few hours she returned to a clean house.

Chapter 10

The house was decorated with balloons and a large banner reading *Happy 2ⁿᵈ Birthday, Maria.* Some children from the neighborhood, both grandmothers, along with Rachel, who was now four and Jimmy, who was three, were eating cake and playing games. Alex came home with a big soft teddy bear.

"Happy birthday, Ria my little dear. Here is your present."

"Thank you, Daddy," she said, throwing her arms around his neck and kissing his cheek.

Then he picked her up and swung her in a circle to Maria's great delight.

"More, Daddy, spin me more."

"Me, too, Daddy," said Jimmy.

He was swung around the room too. Soon all the kids wanted to have a ride.

"That's enough, kids, I'm getting dizzy."

"Alex," Elena said, "I asked Lori and she said it would be fine with her. Can the kids come home and spend the night at my house?"

"Okay with me. Kids, do you want to spend the night at *Abuela's*?"

"Yeah, can we? Can we, Mommy?"

"Good, I'll take them with me. Kids, we have some good movies we can watch together, and we'll play games—"

"Can we go in the pool?" Rachel asked.

"No, it's still too cool and the water is cold."

After everyone had left, the house seemed suddenly vacant. "Now, my sweet, we can have some alone time. Time to get serious and make another baby." Alex said as Lori frowned.

ᴄᴏᴄᴏ

To help her get in the mood, Lori lit candles in the bedroom and put on a CD with soft music. After a shower, she put on a sexy red teddy. Alex too showered and came into the room wearing a silk robe and carrying a bottle of champagne and glasses. He filled the glasses. "Cheers, my sweet."

At first, he was gently kissing her on the lips, the

neck and lower. Then gently he played with her pubic hairs, then he groped, at first, playfully between her legs.

"Aha," he said angrily, and pulled out the IUD. "Now I know why you never got pregnant anymore. You whore, don't you know that it's against our faith?"

"Alex, please, I just could not handle any more babies at this time. Please, understand. It's not that I was against having more kids, I just wanted some spacing." Big tears ran down her cheeks.

"You are going to get it now," he grabbed her knees and pulled them apart.

"Please stop, I'm not ready."

"Well, I'm ready." He entered her while painfully twisting her nipples.

After releasing his semen he got off and viciously slapped her in the face repeatedly.

"I really should bugger you, you no good bitch. I just might after I beat the crap out of you."

"No, please don't beat me. I'll suck it for you."

"Then get down on your knees in front of me and do it."

While they were thus occupied, he reached into the dresser drawer and pulled out a belt. Then he whipped her on the back with the heavy buckle making a nasty wound. Lori jumped up and ran out of the room and down the steps. Alex followed her, the belt still in his hand. Since she was nude she did not want to run outside. She ran into the kitchen, feeling another whack on her back. There she was able to get on the opposite side of the island, and momentarily felt safe. Alex, however swung the belt horizontally and it wrapped around Lorraine's neck. With an evil grin he pulled her toward him. Out of the corner of her eyes she saw the large knife that had been used to cut the birthday cake laying in the sink needing to be washed. She grabbed the knife, plunged it into his stomach, and jerked it up. Alex gave a surprised look and released the belt. Then he grabbed at the knife and fell to the floor. After a few jerks and quivers he was dead.

Lorraine stood there in shock. She looked at him not believing what she saw. *There is a lot of blood on the floor. I hope it won't stain the grout.* She looked out of the kitchen window and saw the wind moving the children's swings. Then she felt chilly and went upstairs to put on some clothes. She saw his blood on her body and went into the shower. She showered until the water turned cold. Then she put on underwear. When she closed her bra she felt the pain on her back. She completed the dressing with slacks and a sweater and jogging shoes. She returned to the kitchen, expecting the floor to be clean and the clean dishes ready to come out of the dishwasher. When she saw the body she gave a startled scream. She went to the linen closet and pulled out a large bath towel and covered the body leaving the head uncovered. She sat on a stool at the counter and looked at the scene on the floor.

"What am I going to do now?" she asked the clock on the wall.

The clock gave no answer. Outside darkness rapidly pushed the day away. She sat on the stool with her face buried in the hands and slumped shoulders. She closed her eyes and thought.

I am so ashamed. Ashamed for having lost my virginity and having to get married. Yes, but I have three beautiful children out of that. Ashamed for covering up bruises he gave me. Did he ever really love me? If he did how could he take a belt to my back like that? How could he make me do things I didn't want to do? Did I really love him that much? Maybe it was just that I felt trapped by circumstances. Married life was not all bad. I live in this beautiful house.

I enjoy being with his family. They are going to hate me now. My children are at their house. Will I ever see them again? Maybe I should just bury the body in the back yard and say he took off. Yeah right, that story wouldn't hold water for a minute. I should call Mom and Dad, they'll tell me what to do. Oh God, how will they take this? Will they ever forgive me? Maybe the easiest would be if I just kill myself. I can't do that, I would go to hell for eternity. I might be going there anyway, so what difference would it make?

The house was dark. The only light came in from the street lamp. She went to turn on lights and draw the drapes shut, took a deep breath, and called her parents.

"Mom, would you and dad please come over here right now. I'm in trouble."

"What kind of trouble?" Mary asked.

"Just come over and be prepared for the worst."

Lori left the kitchen dark. In a few minutes, two very anxious looking people were at her door. Lori let them in, closed the door behind them, and cried. Her parents sat on the couch and watched in silence. After a while Lori composed herself and started to speak.

"Mom, Dad, I did a terrible thing, I don't know what to do now. Please help me."

Mary got up and hugged her daughter. "What could you possibly have done that is so bad?"

Lori sobbed uncontrollably for several minutes before she could speak again. "Alex beat me and I thought he was going to kill me. I grabbed a kitchen knife and stabbed him."

"Oh my God, where is he now? In the hospital.?" Mary asked.

"No, lying in the kitchen."

Both parents rushed into the kitchen, turned on the light, and saw the body covered with a colorful towel and the big lump they figured was the knife. Mary screamed and Lorne clutched his chest. Both of them were pale as they returned to the living room and flopped down on the couch.

"Are you ready to see my back?" Lorraine asked.

Without waiting for an answer, she pulled her sweater up and showed the welts and the marks of the buckle. The belt was still laying on the kitchen floor.

"We should take pictures of that," Lorne said. "Where is your camera?"

"In the drawer over there," Lorraine said, pointing to the console table in the living room.

Lorne took the camera and took several pictures of Lorraine's wounds, but he did not turn on the date feature.

"Now what you have to do, Lori, is call the police," Mary said. "This is clearly a case of self-defense. Get yourself a lawyer and I'm sure you'll get off."

"I don't want to go to jail," Lorraine sobbed. "Mom, call the police for me."

"It will be better if you do it. We'll stay here with you. Everything will be all right," her father assured her.

Soon about a six police cars were gathered in front to the house. Dozens of neighbors milled around in clusters. The police had a job just keeping them from coming into the house.

Lorraine was questioned by two detectives. Photographers took pictures. Eventually, the body was removed. Lorraine was led away in handcuffs and put into a police car.

Both Albrights watched with tears in their eyes. When the police sealed the house, the Albrights headed toward their car through a gauntlet of neighbors.

"We can't talk now," is all Mary told the curious by-

standers. Then they got in the car and drove the short distance home.

Meanwhile, Lorraine was taken to the Yuma jail
where she was fingerprinted, photographed, strip
searched, and told to take a shower. She was given an orange jumpsuit to wear before she was locked in a cell.
She put her back against the wall and felt her knees go
weak. Sliding down the wall until her buttocks touched
the floor, she put her head between her knees and remained like that for the rest of the night.

Chapter 11

Two days later she appeared before the judge for her arraignment and learned her bail had been set at two million dollars. Her parents were in the courtroom. When Lorraine heard the number she looked at her parents and saw the hopeless look on their faces. She knew that there was no way her parents could beg, borrow, or steal the money needed for bail.

Lorraine was hoping to be able to hire a lawyer by making a loan with the equity there was in the house she had been living in for the last nearly five years. Her brother Frank was trying to help there. That's when she found out that the house was in Alexandro's name alone. When all the dust settled, Lorraine learned that she was alone and penniless. She had to ask for a public defender to represent her. Meanwhile, she sat in jail in a cell all alone. The only people on her side were her parents and Frank. Even his wife, Kimberly, whom she had considered a close friend, kept her distance, as if she was contagious with a terrible disease.

A few days later a very young lawyer came to see her. "My name is George Owens, and I'm appointed to represent you. Will you please tell me what happened?"

Lorraine started with the daughter's second birthday party and how angry her husband got when he discovered she had been using birth control. When she said how he made her have oral sex the young man, who looked young enough to be still going to high school, blushed. When she told him how she was beaten with the belt she saw no sign of pity in his eyes. She was at least hoping for a sympathetic ear and possibly a friend. George Owens looked like he could not wait to conclude the interview. When she was escorted back to her cell all she could say to herself was *I'm dead meat. I'll just sit here and die. Why fight it? My life is over. I should have let him kill me.*

Suddenly, time became meaningless. Most of the time she did not even know what month it was. She tried reading, but nothing interested her. When she finished a page and asked herself what she had read, she had no idea. After a while, she would go to the day room and watch television. Nothing appealed to her. Happy shows made her depressed, action shows made her afraid. She drank mostly water. She ate, but everything tasted like chalk. The twenty-four inch waist she had one time wished for, suddenly appeared, but when she did see a reflection in a steel mirror, she hated the sight. Lorraine wished she would simply go to sleep and not wake up. She tried holding her breath and wondered how long it would be before she died, yet somehow she always started breathing. Her lawyer saw her several times more, but she figured the only reason he did so was because it was required by law.

An eternity later, the matron brought her real clothes. "Your mother brought you this, put it on, today is your trial. Let me know when you are dressed and we'll take you to the court house."

With that the woman tossed a bag into the cell. Lorraine put on the navy blue dress, nylons, and high heeled shoes. She combed her shoulder length straight brown hair as best she could, wishing she could have had a stylish cut. *At least that is a little sign of life, I wish for my hair to look better. Like it makes a difference.* After applying a little lipstick, she told the matron that she was ready.

When she entered the court room, she saw her parents. She had to look again and was only sure of who they were because they were sitting next to Frank. Her father looked a good ten years older. He was very pale and the laughter that one had always seen in his blue eyes had been replaced by a dullness, surrounded with dark circles. Her mother's hair that was always neat and shiny red, had grown out into a salt and pepper with some color clinging on the ends. It seemed the weight Lorraine and her father had lost found a home on the mother. The parents nodded in her direction when they made eye contact. Frank smiled and gave a small wave with the hand.

On the prosecution side of the court-room sat her in-laws. Elena looked straight ahead with a hard expression. Next to her was Juan with a clenched jaw and squinting eyes. Near them were other male relatives. All of them were big Hispanic men who looked like hit men for the mafia. Everyone had an *I-dare-you* expression.

The jury entered. There were six men—four of them were Hispanic—and six women. One was Hispanic, one black, and four were white.

George Owens leaned toward Lorraine. "Good news, I got the charge reduced from murder to manslaughter."

"What? I told you it was self-defense."

"The judge would not go for self-defense."

The judge entered dressed in his black robe. Lori suddenly saw black spots dancing in front of her eyes and she used all the will-power she had to keep from fainting. The judge was a friend of the Lopez family.

I'm totally dead meat. The kid might as well just pack up and skate out of here for all the good he is going to do for me.

Before long the trial was concluded. As expected the verdict was guilty and the judge sentenced Lorraine to fifteen years. Two constables took Lorraine into a back room where she could have a few minutes with her parents and Frank.

"You were railroaded," is all her father could say. "Those bastards sold you up the river." He hugged his daughter while the constables looked on suspiciously. "This might be the last time I see you."

"Don't say that Lorne," Mary said with tears streaming down her face. "We'll mount an appeal, we'll get you released."

"That'll never happen in Yuma," Frank claimed. "That Lopez clan has the city by the balls. I don't know how they do it, but I have only sold five cars in the last three months. I will probably move to Phoenix and get a job there."

"Oh Frank, don't do that," said Mary. "Your father and I really need you and Kimberly here, especially now that I can't even see my grandchildren."

"Yes, Mom, what is going on with my children?"

"Elena and Juan have filed for full custody. I hope we will get grandparent's rights to see them."

"Please, Mom, send me pictures of the kids and of you and Dad and Frank and Kim and the baby when it's born."

"Time's up," interjected the constable.

The Albright family made a group hug to the dismay of the younger constable. The older man seemed to sympathize with Lorraine and her family. Then she was cuffed and taken away. She left with her head held high.

"We'll pray for you," was the last statement she heard from her father.

The bus ride to Goodyear seemed to last forever. She sat in the dull gray bus with her arms and legs shackled to the floor. In the bus were about a dozen other men and women in the same position. A guard with a gun sat watching them. A steel screen separated them from the driver.

Lori watched as the night settled over the desert on the three hour ride to her new home.

As soon as I get there, I'll take the first opportunity to kill myself. This is not a human way to live. I don't even wish this on the meanest animal. Oh, Alex, I tried so hard to be a good wife to you. Why, why, why did this have to happen? Why did you take such pleasure in causing pain? Damn you, I hope it really hurt when I plunged the knife into you. How many girls are at this moment suffering the same abuse? No telling, most of them cover it up, just like I did.

On Route 85 the bus pulled over to the left and into the prison complex. They stopped near a low gray building. Guards came aboard and took off the men. When the bus moved again the driver yelled cheerfully, "Perryville next stop."

Perryville, what a cheerful sounding name for such a dismal place. How will I manage to cope there? What am I thinking? I'll cope by just killing myself. How? I don't know yet, I'll figure it out. I should just have committed hari-kari when I had the chance. Oh, sweet Jesus, help me. Help me to wake up from this nightmare. I wish that's all it was, just a bad dream.

The bus stopped near a low building and the women were unshackled. They were led in, again photographed, and strip searched. Then they were told to take a shower and put on an orange jumpsuit. She was led past a row of cells with women who called greetings. Some friendly, many obscene. Then she was locked in a cell containing a narrow cot, a steel toilet and a sink.

"There's home sweet home," mocked the guard. "We're going to keep our eyes on you. We would not want anything to happen to you. Good night and pleasant dreams."

Lorraine cautiously sat on the bed, waiting to be attacked by bed bugs. When that did not happen she crawled under the rough blanket and closed her eyes. Slowly she became aware of the sounds of the prison. She heard toilets being flushed, women crying, snoring, and one was praying out loud. *I'll never get used to this place. I have to get out of here, one way or another.*

The human being is an amazing animal. Lori actually got used to the routine of the prison. At first, she was confined to her cell for most of the day. She could get out to shower and go to the library. She even found books that interested her.

She wrote lengthy letters to her parents and brother.

She wrote letters to her children which she doubted they would ever receive. After being confined for a few months, she was visited by her brother.

"Frank, I'm so happy to see you," she said through the plexiglass pane separating them.

"Sis, how are you doing?" Frank asked with a sad expression.

"Believe it or not, I think I'm actually getting used to this place. Why so sad?"

"Lori, I have bad news."

"Oh, what is it?"

"Dad, he had a heart attack and died yesterday."

"No, Frank, not Dad. Where did he die? How is Mom taking it?"

"He was taking his morning walk and collapsed on a neighbor's lawn. The paramedics came and tried to revive him, but it was too late. Mom is still in shock. As of a few hours ago, she is going about like nothing happened. All she does is talk about the little motorhome they had just bought and where they are planning on going. Dad was so depressed, that Mom suggested he go and buy the motorhome he had always wanted. It was financed, but fortunately they took out an insurance policy, so it will be paid off."

"When will the funeral be?"

"Day after tomorrow."

"Oh, Frank, I wish I could go. Do you think you could talk to them to let me attend?"

"I already asked about that and the answer is a definite no."

"Oh, Frank, do you think I deserve this?"

"No Sis, you don't deserve this."

"And the next line will be, God works in mysterious ways and good will come out of this."

"You said it, Sis. Now keep your eyes and ears open and take every opportunity coming your way."

"I'll do that, Frank. Now tell me about your family while we still have time."

Frank pulled out some photographs and showed them through the glass. "Here is a picture of Zachary when he was born, and this is how he looks now at three months."

"Beautiful baby, give him a kiss for me."

"And here is a picture of Kimberly taken last week."

"I see she still has a few pounds to shed."

"She's working at it."

"How's the new job going?"

"Well, as I wrote to you, since we moved to Phoenix things have worked out for us. I'm again selling cars and doing well. Now that Mom's alone I feel bad we live so far away. Maybe I can get her to come and live in Phoenix too, then she could come and visit you more often."

"I doubt if that will happen. She is so involved in church and with her friends and various clubs."

"And every day she combs the newspaper for any article relating to the Lopezes. She finally got visitation rights with your children. It's only once a month for a measly two hours and supervised, but she says that is better than nothing."

"I hope she takes pictures of them."

"She will, and mail them to you."

"I miss my children more than anything. To get a visit from them would be too much to hope for." With a frown she continued. "On the other hand, I would not want them to see me here like this."

"Time is up," called the guard.

"Good bye, Frank, thank you for coming. Give Mom a big hug for me and tell her I love her very much."

"I will. Bye, Sis," Frank said as he quickly left.

She did not see the tears in his eyes.

Chapter 12

Lorraine stayed out of trouble and as time went by she slowly received privileges. When she had the opportunity for vocational training, she eagerly took it. She figured there was always need for auto mechanics. Since she did not mind getting her hands dirty, she jumped at the chance to learn that trade. After a few years, she took the exam for certification and passed it with flying colors. After that, she worked in the motor pool for which she was paid fifty cents an hour. That enabled her to be able to send her mother money as a gift for Christmas, her birthday, and Mother's Day. She also would send some money to Frank for his two children, which the parents put into bank accounts for them.

According to the letters her mother had written, none

of her children received any letters or cards she had sent them. So she stopped trying to correspond with them. Most of her earnings she put into a bank account. To see the balance grow gave her a small amount of pleasure. It was the first time in her life she had her own money. The day her deposit reached one thousand dollars she celebrated silently.

After working all day on cars and trucks she was happy to sit down to a meal without having to cook. Cooking was not her favorite thing to do, even though she had managed to put satisfactory meals on the table while married to Alex. Then she went back to her cell, which she considered her little sanctuary. When she was told that she had earned the privilege of living in a dorm, she was not happy about it.

"How many women are in a dorm?" She asked the matron.

"Ten."

"I have to sleep with nine other women? Do I have a choice in the matter?"

"Everyone thinks it is better than the cells. You'll have more privileges too, like outdoor time and use of the facilities. Try it, you might just like it."

After a period of adjustment, Lorraine did not mind too much being in the dorm. In the cells, she could hear the other women's bodily noises, too. One cell neighbor was very skilled at making loud flagellations, accompanied by loud laughter, and asking if everyone heard it.

That really annoyed Lorraine and she was glad to get away from her.

In the dormitory, Lorraine had room to hang up her pictures. Her roommates looked at them with interest and asked her about her family. She simply said that she did not want to talk about them. "It just is too painful."

To her surprise, over the years she actually made several friends. When one of her friends was released it was a bitter sweet time. She was happy for them, but sad at losing them.

"I'll write," was a general promise. "You have to come and see me when you get out."

Few kept their promise to write, even Lorraine's letters remained unanswered.

One day while she was at the hairdresser who came in to do the women, Lorraine was told that she had quite a few gray hairs.

"In that case, give me a short haircut. I never did like to see long gray hair."

"Are you sure. It really is not that many hairs."

"I should have gotten a short cut a long time ago. Give me a crew cut."

"A crew cut, are you sure?"

"I'm sure. It's only hair, it'll grow back."

"Okay, here goes, one crew cut coming up."

Lorraine did not have to comb her hair for a long time after that.

The years passed faster and faster. For some unknown reason there was never a parole hearing. She celebrated her thirty-seventh birthday in jail. Someone had put a candle in a donut and everyone sang "Happy Birthday" to her that morning.

"Thank you, and I love all of you, but I hope this is my last birthday in dear old Perryville."

"Hey, don't talk about leaving us," said her friend Lilly, "stay here until all our time is up."

"I'll miss you girls, too, but no use talking about that now, let me open the present you are giving me."

Wrapped in a bag with tissue paper was a lipstick, some eye liner, and foundation.

"We know you stopped wearing make-up, but when you get out, I'm sure there are some men eager to meet you."

"The only men eager to meet me will be guys whose cars need fixing. I can just see them now giving me a hard look and thinking, 'A woman? What the heck does she know about cars?' Then I'll point to the grade I got on the certification test and tell them that they have to be patient with me because I only got a score of ninety-eight."

All the girls laughed. "You tell them, girlfriend," said Lilly.

❦

On the day of her release, the women prisoners gave

her hugs and teary farewells. Most were encouraging, a few were pessimistic, telling her she would not know how to cope on the outside. After dressing in street clothes that were not orange in color, she went to the bank window and received a check for several thousand dollars. When she received her personal belongings, she put her one carat diamond ring on her right hand and slipped the wedding band in a purse. Then she walked into a reception area where Frank was waiting for her. Together they stepped into a warm but windy March day.

Frank's wife Kimberly was in a second car with Lorraine's two nephews. They got out of the car and walked toward her as Frank escorted her to his car.

"Lori, how good to see you."

Lorraine gave her a cool greeting. "I'm surprised you are here. All these years you never came once to see me. All I saw of you and the boys were pictures."

"Frank told me how depressing it was to see you in jail."

"Not nearly as depressing as actually living there. Another thing, I'm no longer Lori. Lori is the little girl and the abused wife. I am Lorraine. Now please, call me only that."

"Yes, Lori—I mean Lorraine. Forgive me if I slip some times. And please, forgive me for never coming for a visit. Here are Zachary and Matt, your nephews," Kimberly said as two young teen aged boys approached. "Come boys, say hello to your Aunt Lorraine."

"Hello, Aunt Lorraine," said the boys, shaking her hand.

"Give your aunt a hug," said Frank.

Lorraine saw the boy's reluctance. "That's okay boys. There will be time for that later."

"Zach, what were you going to tell your aunt?"

"Thank you for the gifts of money, both Matt and I have it in the bank."

"Yes, you boys always wrote nice thank you notes, I really appreciate that."

"I'm on the way to take the boys to baseball practice." interjected Kimberly. "We'll get together another time."

"That's okay, I'm glad you came here for a meeting, even if it was short. Good bye, I'm eager to get to Yuma and see Mom." She turned to Frank. He took her by the hand and escorted her to the car."

When they neared Yuma, Lorraine could not believe how much the town had grown. Where there was only desert when she last was there, houses dotted the landscape as if they had been dropped out of the sky. Between the houses it was green with trees.

"Yuma has grown to three Wal-Marts now," Frank said.

"Three? How many K-Marts?"

"That closed up years ago."

"Too bad, I always liked K-Mart."

They arrived in the old residential section of Yuma, a

neighborhood that looked the same. When Frank parked in front of their mother's house, Lorraine felt butterflies in her stomach but also a heaviness around the heart. She took a deep breath as Frank opened the door for her and led her into the house. The aroma of roast beef greeted them.

When Mary heard them enter, she rushed from the kitchen into the living room. "Lori," she said with outstretched arms. "My dear Lori,"

Lorraine hardly recognized the old woman in front of her. It seemed like not only did her girth widen but her height shrank. Her hair was totally white and her eyes were draped with valances. The once smooth skin was furrowed with hundreds of wrinkles.

"Mom, oh, Mom," was all she managed to say as she fell into the embrace. They held each other for a good minute or two.

"Lori, let me look at you," Mary said as she stepped back. "I like your hair like that, looks easy to keep."

"Yes Mom, I got tired of having to mess with long hair."

"Dinner is almost ready. Come in the kitchen and give me a hand. Frank, you want to set the table in the dining room?"

"Sure Mom, which dishes you want me to use?"

"I sold the good china. All I've got is the old everyday dishes."

"You mean you sold the set you got as a wedding

present. If I would have known that, Kim and I would have bought it."

"I did not think you two wanted it. Sorry, I should have asked. No big deal, it was only dishes. That is not that important in life."

Mom has surely changed, I remember the time I accidentally broke a plate and she flew off the handle for me being clumsy. She is right, dishes are not that important.

The three sat down at the dining room table. Lorraine enjoyed eating off china and using stainless flatware with real knifes. She had almost forgotten what a real knife looked like. All she had seen the last many years were plastic knifes. The dinner was like the nectar of the gods.

"Delicious dinner, Mom. Thank you so much for cooking it."

"I have really cut back on my cooking. With no one to share the meal with, why do much effort in cooking? When I eat with company, we just go out and everybody pays their own."

"How are things in church?"

"Very active. There are a lot of new members. I did go when your children had Holy Communion. I still have visitation once a month, but the only one in town is Maria and she acts like she doesn't want to see me. Rachel is now a sophomore in some college in Texas and Jimmy was accepted in the Naval Academy no less. He's been there since July last year."

"That is an interesting fact no one bothered to mention to me," Lorraine said, a bit annoyed.

"Oh, I thought I sent you the newspaper article from the *Yuma Sun*. I must have forgotten. I have all newspaper articles referring to the family. Rachel was Miss Yuma County two years ago."

"Yes, I got that article. And what can you tell me about Maria?"

"She is a senior in high school."

"Which school is she going to?"

"St Francis parochial school. All the children went to Catholic school. That is something I could never have afforded. Lori—"

"Please call me Lorraine. Lori is the frightened person in my past. Lorraine's the new woman who will get a job and make a living on her own."

"You will live here with me?" Mary asked anxiously.

"I'll stay a few nights. How have the neighbors been treating you?"

"It has never been the same," was all she said.

"Lorraine, will you be buying a car?" Frank, the car sales man, asked eagerly.

"Give me time, I don't know yet."

"Lori—Lorraine you can drive mine for a while. It runs pretty good, even with a knock."

"If it has a knock, I can fix that."

"I see you still have that motorhome you bought almost fifteen years ago," Frank said. "It's a shame just sitting there deteriorating. You should have sold it years ago."

"Should have, would have, could have, that's all I'm ever told. That was the last thing your father bought. We were going to start a new life with it."

"Let me see that motorhome," Lorraine said eagerly.

"We'll look at it after dinner, now finish your meal. I got some strawberry short cake for dessert."

"I'm full, Mom, later it will taste good. Come, let's see the motorhome."

Mary took the keys off the hook and went into the back yard where the rig was parked.

It was a twenty-two foot class-C Jamboree. The first thing Lorraine noticed was that the tires had hardly been used, but definitely needed replacing. The interior was not bad, considering it had been sitting for so many years. There was some de-lamination of the Formica. *I can fix that.* In the back was a double bed with a good mattress on it. There was a bathroom with shower and sink and the kitchen had a stove with oven and a small double sink. The cabinets were more adequate in space than Lorraine had lived with for fifteen years.

"Does it run?"

"I haven't started it for years," Mary said.

"Then the batteries are dead. Mom, if I fix it up, would you let me use it?"

"There was a time I wanted to travel in it, but no more. What would you like to do with it?"

"I would like to see the USA. After what I have been through, that would be good therapy. I don't feel safe living in the same town as the Lopezes and I don't want to see the house I used to live in. What I really need is to get away. To see beautiful scenery, to be where no one knows me and to find myself."

"You a psychiatrist now?"

"No, but I am an auto mechanic."

"Hey, Sis, I think that would be a great idea. I wish I could go with you, but I have responsibilities. You wouldn't want me and the family along, now would you?"

"No, I wouldn't."

"That was a quick answer," Frank said.

"You know, I think that would be a good thing for you to do, Lori—since I have been calling you Lori for thirty-seven years, I can't suddenly change."

"Okay, Mom, you are the only one to whom I am Lori. Now Frank can remember I'm Lorraine. But he mostly calls me Sis anyway. That's okay, Frank, I'm proud to be your sis."

"Frank, it's getting late, are you planning on returning to Phoenix tonight?"

"You know, Mom, if you don't mind, I'd like to go and get a bottle of wine so we can sit here and celebrate Lorraine's return to the family. I took tomorrow off, anyway. It's been a long time since I slept in my old room."

"You might as well take advantage of it. I was thinking of selling the house and going into an apartment in a senior housing project. One of my friends lives there, and they are really nice."

"Can you afford the rent?" Frank wanted to know.

"Well, first I'll sell the house and the rent is assessed according to income."

"Mom, are you old enough for senior living?" Lorraine asked.

"I'm getting up there. I'm sixty-four, you know."

"Well, you don't look it," Frank said cheerfully.

"Yeah, I know, I look eighty-four."

"Whatever age you look, you are beautiful," Lorraine said. "And you don't look eighty-four, just a mature sixty."

"Let me just run to the store and get some wine," Frank interjected. "Any preference, Sis, since it's your party."

"How about a white wine? Or a white Zin?"

"Will do. I'll be back soon."

"Lori, help me clear the table, would you?"

"Sure, Mom."

Soon Frank returned with two bottles of wine. They sat in the small living room with the drapes tightly drawn. "I don't like anyone to see me in the house at night," Mary said.

"Good idea. Sometimes things happen because someone sees a woman in the house alone," Frank said.

"When would it be good for me to bring up Kim and the boys for a visit?"

"You know any time would be good, just let me know you are coming so I can have food prepared."

"We would like to come up some times and just take you out to dinner."

"I would like that."

"Tell you what. I'll bring the family up Sunday, okay with you?"

"That'll be fine, and then we can go out to eat. Would you like that, Lori?"

"Love it."

They sat up late into the night, talking and enjoying glasses of wine.

"It has been years since I have had a drink," Lorraine said.

"You might have enjoyed going to a bar," Frank said.

"No way. All that noise and strange people? I'm just not ready for that. A quiet evening with my family is just what the doctor ordered. I'm quite content just being with you."

"We are so glad to have you back home." Mary sighed. "If only your father would have lived to see the day. He died way too young, over fourteen years ago."

"I know, Mom, and the sad part was I could not even come to his funeral."

Suddenly everyone took on a sad face.

"Dad always enjoyed a glass of wine," Frank said,

raising his glass. "Here's to you, Dad, where ever you are. We still love you."

"Here, here," the others said and took a sip from their glasses.

Chapter 13

It took Lorraine the rest of March before she had the motorhome in running condition again. After buying insurance and a license plate from the DMV, she also got a new driver's license for herself.

By the first of April, the traffic in Yuma had visibly decreased as many of the snowbirds were leaving or had already gone north.

"Mom, if you don't mind I would like to sleep in the motorhome. I need to get used to it."

"Then one day I'll look out and you will be gone with the rig."

"No, Mom, I won't sneak off on you. Are you sure you don't just want to close up the house and come with me?"

"No, dear, I get carsick. You go with my blessings, but promise not to sneak away."

"I promise."

"What are you going to do if you run out of money?"

"I have a few thousand left, even after spending over two thousand getting the rig road ready. If I get low on funds, I'll try to get a job."

"You know, Lori, I've been thinking, since you put all that money into the vehicle, how about I sell it to you."

"I don't know if I can afford to buy it."

"Of course you can, I'll give it to you at a good price."

"How much is that?"

"How about one dollar?"

"I think I can afford that. Gee thanks, Mom," she said, giving her mother a hug and kiss.

"If you have time today, we could go to DMV and take care of it right away."

"That'll be fine. I have no better plans for this afternoon."

That evening Lorraine sat alone in her motorhome and drank a glass of wine. *It's mine, all mine. This is the first time I've actually owned something. What a great thing to own. I can live in it, I can cruise with it. I can park wherever I want.* She looked at a road map of the USA. *Hello, America, you are now my back yard.*

Lorraine was delighted to discover a 99-Cent Store. There she bought dishes and canned goods. A trip to Wal-Mart rounded out everything else she needed. She put everything away and still had room to spare.

That evening over supper she told Mary, "Mom, my rig is stocked up and gassed up. I really don't see any reason to keep hanging around here."

"But, Lori, you've only been home for a month and—"

"I know. You said you saw my daughter Maria and she wants nothing to do with me."

"Wait a few more weeks. Maybe next time I can talk her into agreeing to see you."

"And if she says no, then what? Mom, being here in this neighborhood is painful for me. Just this afternoon, I found myself driving by *the* house and I burst out crying. Please, Mom, understand. I really need to get away from here. The sooner the better."

"Well, in that case, I too have made up my mind. I will put the house on the market tomorrow. I hope for a quick sale and then I'll move into the senior apartments. Now when you are on the road, you will stay in touch with me?"

"Of course, Mom. You have my cell number. I'll call you every day, unless I'm out of range which I under-stand happens sometimes. So if you don't hear from me for a day or so, don't worry."

"Oh, Lori, my dear girl, I'll miss you. It was nice

having someone in the house again. And now you want to take off."

"Yes, Mom, that's just something I have to do."

⟨⟩⟨⟩

Since Mary was in the habit of sleeping late, and Lorraine liked to get up early, the two women said their farewells in the evening. At the first sign of daylight, Lorraine pulled the rig out of the yard and headed toward I-8 going east. When the rising sun was in her eyes, she pulled over into a rest stop and made herself breakfast. Sitting at the table in the privacy of her rig, she looked out of the large window and enjoyed the sight of the purple verbena and yellow daisy-like blooms of the brittle bush.

"Heaven, this is heaven. I can do what I like whenever I like. No strict rules to follow, no guards yelling at me. No noise from all the other people. Just me by myself, enjoying my own company. I was badly hurt, but I will overcome."

Just then a car pulled up and parked near the rig. A family with three small children got out. The father carried the smallest one, a boy of about two, in his arms toward the rest room. The mother had two little girls by the hand going in the same direction. Seeing this happy family made her sad.

That could have been me. I wonder where they are

going. Maybe I'll see them down the road again.

She took a deep breath, put the empty coffee mug in the sink, and took her seat behind the wheel. She did not want to see the happy family get back into their car. Quickly she left the parking lot of the rest stop.

Lorraine had planned on stopping in Tucson, but driving through the traffic to get some gas was enough for her. She did not want to be in congestion. She got back on I-10 and continued east. By the time she reached Deming, New Mexico, she was ready to cease driving for the day. By sheer luck, the campground she chose to go to was a LoW camp ground.

"Welcome to the campground," said the white haired man behind the desk in the office. He chuckled. "Are you a low-life?"

"What?"

"Are you a member of Loners on Wheels?"

"No, I'm new to RV-ing and I have never heard of Loners on Wheels."

"We are an RV club for people traveling alone. With membership, you get discounts at many RV parks. Would you like to sign up? We also have many jamborees all over the USA. It's a lot of fun."

"How much is the membership?"

"$45.00 for the year. But you can save the first ten dollars per night right here."

"Sounds great, if you'll have me, I'm ready to join."

"Just fill out this brief membership application, pay

me the dues, and you are a member of the club. Tonight we're having a dance at the club house. You be sure you come."

"Thank you. I'll be glad to come, provided I don't have to bring a dance partner."

"Partner not required. There are plenty of men who would love to dance with you."

Lorraine just had time for a quick shower and to put on a colorful full skirt and blouse before the dance started. Her apprehension on entering the hall alone was unfounded. The fifty or so men and women saw that she was a stranger and went up to greet her.

"Come, there is an empty chair next to me," said one man in his sixties. "Can I get you a glass of wine or some soda?"

"Wine would be lovely."

"Red or white?"

"Whatever, but white preferably."

Soon he returned with a clear plastic cup full of white wine. "My name is Ray, What's yours?"

"I'm Lorraine."

"You ready for a spin on the dance floor?" he asked when a two-step was playing on the CD player.

"I'd love to. Just want to warn you that I haven't danced in a while. My dancing might be rusty."

"Hey, you're talking to someone with two left feet."

Ray took her hand and led her to the open space called a dance floor. He put his arm on her back in a closed dance position and they moved to the music.

My God, if he knew how long it has been since a man touched me other than my brother. He probably would consider me contaminated and run the other way.

"You're a good dancer, I like dancing with you."

"Thank you," she said. "And your two left feet are well coordinated."

When the music ended, every one grabbed another partner to dance with. Before the evening was over, Lorraine felt she had a bunch of new friends. It felt good to be among people who did not care where she came from or what her background was. People were not even interested in her last name. If they asked where she was from, they were only interested in telling her that they had been there, too. The name Lopez meant nothing to them. When the dance was over, Ray walked her back to her motorhome and even gave her a small kiss on the lips.

"Hope to see you in the morning for coffee in the lounge."

"Thank you. I had more fun than you know. Good night."

Ray could be classified a dirty old man since he is so much older than me, but damn, it was nice to have the attention and even a little kiss. Maybe there is hope for me yet. She crawled under the soft blanket with a happy smile on her face.

❧❧❧

The next morning there were about a dozen men and women in the lounge drinking coffee and exchanging news.

"I was hoping to get underway this morning, but she wouldn't start," lamented a man called Warren. "I really do need to get to Texas for my grandson's college graduation. If I don't get there in three days, I'll miss the big event. Does anyone know a good mechanic in town?"

"Is it gas or diesel?" Lorraine asked.

"Gas."

"Would you mind if I have a look at your rig?"

He gave her a *what-do-you-know? You're-a-woman* look.

"I know a little about motors," she said.

"Okay, you can see it. No harm in that."

After they drank their coffee, they went together to look at his motorhome.

"Has the trouble been off and on or just sudden?"

"No, I never had the trouble before."

When Lorraine tried, unsuccessfully, to start it she used ether. When that didn't work she came to the conclusion that it was the starter rather than the more serious problem of a fuel pump.

"We could go to an auto supply store and get a starter. I would be glad to put it on for you."

"Really? You can do that?"

"Sure, I'm a certified mechanic and I have tools in my storage bin."

Seeing the hood up on Warren's motorhome brought an assembly of men. They listened to Lorraine and nodded in agreement. "I can drive you both to the Napa store to get the starter," Ray volunteered.

A short time later the new starter was on and the engine purring like a contented cat.

"Lorraine, I insist on paying you for the job," Warren said.

"I'm not charging you, but if you insist, give me whatever you feel is fair."

"Thank you so much. You are a life saver," Warren said, slipping some paper money into her hand. "Now I better get going, Texas is a huge state and I really hope to get there at least one day before graduation." He hopped into his class-A motorhome and drove off, waving happily.

"I have a knock in my engine," said a man she had danced with the previous night. "Could you see what it is and if you can fix it? I certainly don't expect you to work for nothing."

The next six days Lorraine was busy all day, working on motorhomes, motor cycles, and golf carts. When she counted her money, she saw she was over $900.00 richer. She also got great pleasure helping people and seeing their appreciative faces. When she was invited to a potluck, everyone insisted that there would be plenty of food without her contributing. She was to be their honored guest.

A week later, every motor in the park was purring. "I suppose my job here is done for now. I want to shove off and see the country."

"When you get to Wisconsin, you simply have to come and see me," said Ruth, a middle-aged widow. "Here is my address and phone number. Give me a call when you get near."

"Thank you. I might do that."

"And I have a home in Wichita, Kansas. I would love if you come to visit. You can park your rig in my yard." said another lone traveler.

"I live with my son and family on their ranch in Wyoming," Ray said, handing her his contact information.

"Thank you, so much, all of you. You're all just wonderful and I might be able to stop by. One never knows."

Lorraine got into her rig and slowly drove out of the park. Her new friends were waving and wishing her a good journey. Tears came to her eyes before she got back onto I-10 going east.

Suddenly, life felt worth living.

Chapter 14

Lorraine knew that her daughter Rachel was a sophomore at a college in Texas. She looked at the map and saw that San Marcos was a small town near Austin. *Good, that looks like it will be a small school. It should be easy to find my way around that.*

To her surprise, the college consisted of nearly 500 acres and hundreds of buildings. *How the heck will I ever find anyone here?* Lorraine wondered as she found a place in a parking lot. There were thousands of students milling about. She asked one student where the administration building was and was directed, with much pointing and twists and turns of the hands.

"Thank you for your help," she said. *I'm sure I'll need to ask again farther along.*

When she entered the building, she told a reception-
ist that she was trying to locate Rachel Lopez. After a
long time, the woman got Rachel on the phone and told
her that her mother was here to see her. Lorraine saw a
strange expression on the woman's face before she hung
up.

"I'm sorry, ma'am, but she said, and I quote, 'There
is no way I want to see *that* woman.' Then she hung up.
Whatever the problem is, I hope she gets over it soon.
I'm very sorry. If my daughter said that to me, I would
simply be devastated."

"Thank you for your help."

"I'm sorry," the woman said again. "Maybe you can
come back in a few days and she will have gotten over
it."

"I'll do that. Thanks again, and good bye."

The phone rang and the woman answered it as Lorraine left.

She walked back to her motorhome, took a deep
breath, and drove off. "I'll just go to the LoW camp
ground not too far from here."

At the campground, she was warmly greeted by
strangers, had a pleasant evening dancing at the rec hall,
and enjoyed the fellowship over coffee the next morning.
She even was able to help someone with some minor car
repairs for which she was generously rewarded.

*If my family doesn't like me, I'll just enjoy the com-
pany of strangers, where I'm accepted without question.*

The only thing that can hurt me is what I allow to hurt me. And I refuse to be hurt any more.

~~~

After two days of rest at the campground she drove on I-10 going east. She was surprised to learn that the state of Florida had two time zones. The panhandle reached that far west.

Beyond Jacksonville, she laid her eyes on the Atlantic Ocean for the first time. The day in early May was warm and the sand felt warm and soft. She put on a bathing suit and slowly went in the water, only to rush back out when a big wave splashed her. The water was surprisingly cold. She found a camp ground overlooking the ocean. She lay in bed, had a glass of wine, and watched the light fade over the Atlantic. She wondered what it would feel like to be on a ship on the ocean. Then, on the horizon, she saw a sailboat heading north, its white sails tinted pink by the sunset.

Would I have the courage to be out on a small boat like that on this big ocean? Hell, yes. I would jump at the chance to do that.

Lorraine's next objective was to get to Annapolis and the Naval Academy. She had never in her life imagined such an amount of traffic as there was on I-95. The large space between vehicles as one saw west of the Mississippi River was reduced to, "If there is space to squeeze in, it's mine to take." All Lorraine could say to the small cars on the road was, "I'm bigger than you, you better watch out for me."

Of course, they did not hear her say that.

Looking at the map, Route 301 looked like a nice way to go. It went through small towns of Maryland. Soon, however, she was sorry. She had never seen so many red lights in her life. Slowly she crept toward the city of Annapolis.

I expected San Marcos College to be small. I suppose the Naval Academy is really big.

She drove in the entrance near the waterfront. The guard told her she was allowed to park during the day, but could not spend the night.

"That suits me fine," she told him.

"Just be sure you leave by six p.m."

"Thanks."

She parked overlooking Annapolis Harbor surrounded by marinas with pleasure boats. Many small yachts were moored in the harbor, and people were rowing or motoring around in their dinghies. *This time, I will fortify myself with some lunch. If this turns out to be a good day, I will go and celebrate by going to a restaurant for supper and ordering a Maryland specialty.*

The only pictures Lorraine had seen of her children were the ones taken by her mother who was a terrible photographer. It was impossible to make out any detail on the postcard-sized or smaller pictures. When she saw the midshipmen scurrying about the relatively small campus, going to classes, she knew she would never be able to pick out her son. She learned that the freshmen were called plebes. They were easy to spot from the upper class men because they were dressed in all white sailor suits. At the visitor center, she learned that all 4000 mid-shipmen were housed in one large dormitory building. When she asked the lady how she could best find her son, Lorraine was told to go to administration office located near the library. With a map of the campus in hand, Lor-raine walked there.

"We don't allow the plebes to get visitors at any time," said the middle-aged secretary at the front desk. "You might arrange to meet with your son on Saturday afternoon when he is free to leave the campus."

"But this is only Tuesday. I have come all the way from Arizona. I have not seen my son since he was three years old. I'm afraid his paternal grandparents have poi-soned him against me and he does not want to see me at all." Tears came to Lorraine's eyes. She wiped them and took a deep breath.

The secretary looked at her with compassion. She picked up the phone and spoke with the superintendent. "The superintendent has agreed to see you. Just go in that door," she said, pointing to a mahogany door.

"Thank you so much,"

In about two minutes, Lorraine told the officer, who she later found out was a rear admiral dressed in the white navy summer uniform, about her life and the fact that she had been incarcerated for the past fifteen years.

"I'll tell what I'll do," said the rear admiral with kind blue eyes, "I'll send notice to your son to come to my office. Now when he comes in here, don't be surprised to see one very scared young man. He will speak with you, even if I have to order him to."

"Thank you, sir, I am so grateful."

Lorraine remained in the super's office, waiting. It took about a half an hour before a very anxious looking plebe entered.

He did not see his mother sitting against the wall behind him.

"You needed to see me, sir?"

"Yes, Mr. Lopez, there is someone here to see you." He pointed toward Lorraine.

The young man turned around and all Lorraine could say was, "You look just like my father."

"Is that you, Mother?"

"Yes, Jimmy, it's me in person."

In front of her stood a tall, handsome, clean-cut young man with light brown hair and large blue eyes. He stood there, as if carved out of marble, and speechless. He could have been knocked over with a feather.

"Aren't you going to speak to your mother," the superintendent asked. Jaime was still speechless. "Young man, you are training to be a naval officer. It won't do for you to be petrified."

Jaime approached his mother with his right hand extended. "Good to see you, Mother."

"Young man, if you think it's unmanly to hug one's mother," said the rear admiral, "you are mistaken. I have to leave the office for a while. Now sit down and talk with your mother."

"Yes sir, thank you, sir."

The two just stared at each other for a good minute. "Jimmy, my dear Jimmy, you can't imagine how happy I am to see you. How are you? How do you like the Naval Academy?"

"I am well, Mother. Are you really my mother? I have a faint memory of you with long, light brown hair. The last time I saw you was on Maria's second birthday. Then after that my world changed."

"Jimmy, I just really need to tell you that I thought your father was going to kill me. It was strictly self-defense. Please believe me."

"I came to that conclusion by myself. When Grandma Albright came for a visit, she was always supervised. After a while, I figured that they wanted to make sure that never a word in your defense would come out. I figured they had something to hide."

"Did the Lopez family treat you children good?"

"Oh, yes, Grandma Lopez acted like she was our mother. Sometimes she even introduced us as her children. But we did miss you terribly at first. Rachel cried every night, then stopped when she was threatened with

severe punishment. After a while, no one, other than
Grandma Albright mentioned your name. Oh, Mom, I'm
so glad you are out and came to see me. I'll write to you,
I promise."

"Jimmy, there is one thing I have been waiting for
years to do, please let me do it now."

"I can guess." He rose and went into his mother's
outstretched arms. They held each other for a long time.
Lorraine used all of her self-control to not cry for joy.
The two were still hugging when the superintendent returned to the room.

"Now that's more like it, Mr. Lopez."

"When might I be able to see Jaime again?"

"He has to remain on campus till Saturday afternoon,
then he is free until Sunday evening. Do you think you
can stay around until then?"

"I am free to stay wherever I like," Lorraine said
cheerfully. "What do you say, Jimmy? Want to hang
around with your mother?"

"I would be honored and privileged to hang around
with my mother. Where are you staying?"

"I have my motorhome I'm staying in. I'll just find a
camp ground nearby until I can see you again on Saturday."

"There aren't any commercial campgrounds nearby,"
the superintendent said. "But the academy has one, and I
can arrange for you to park there for a few days if that
would be agreeable with you."

"That would be terrific."

"I'll call and make arrangements. My secretary will give you a map and this young man has classes to attend."

"Good bye, Mother, I'll see you Saturday then." And Jaime rushed out of the room.

Lorraine could not remember ever feeling such joy and happiness as she did when she left the super's office. She felt as if she was walking on a cloud. She went into the visitor center and bought some post cards, tee shirts, and a sweat shirt with a big Naval Academy logo on it. She sang out loud.

Her voice cracked on occasion because it had been years since a tune had crossed her lips. She drove around Annapolis, looking for a parking space. No easy feat, especially for a motorhome. She finally found one on a marina parking lot. Then she walked around, looking at colonial houses and buildings. She checked out some little shops and got some souvenir Christmas ornaments for her mother and Frank and family.

By late afternoon, she got hungry and did what she'd promised herself. She went into a restaurant and asked the waitress what was a good Maryland delicacy today.

"We have some soft crabs today."

"I'll try that, I have never eaten soft crabs."

"You are in for a treat. Would you like the typical french fries and coleslaw with it? Our fries are really good."

"Sure, give me all the calories and cholesterol you can manage. And serve it with some wine. Today I'm celebrating."

"What is the occasion, if I may ask?"

"I visited my son at the Naval Academy."

"Congratulations on having a kid in the academy. I'm sure you must be very proud."

"More than you can imagine."

"Soft crab and wine coming up."

The days, until she could meet Jaime at an agreed upon spot were as long as the days before Christmas to little children.

Jaime wore sporty civilian clothes as he climbed into the motorhome. He looked around,

"Where did you get this rig?"

"It's the one my father bought shortly before he died. It has been sitting in their back yard for fifteen years without going anywhere. I fixed it up and am now doing what your grandfather did not live to do."

"Good for you, Mom. I'm sure he is with you."

"Strange you should say that. There are times when I feel my father, and sometimes it seems he is talking to me. We have fifteen years to make up for. Now you have to tell me all about yourself, how school went, and anything else. But first, would you like to go anywhere special today?"

"It's a bit late to drive to Washington, but if you are game, why don't we drive over the bay bridge to the

Eastern Shore and go to a restaurant? I would like to eat without having to sit at attention."

"Maybe we could even get some soft crabs again?"

"Great idea, so you like them."

"I never thought I would like to eat a big spider."

"Hey, Mom, considering that you are a Yuma gal, you really are cool."

"Whatever you mean by that, I'll take it as a compliment. Thank you."

The going was slow, waiting to get to the toll both to pay for the use of the bridge. Finally they were able to drive over the hanging bridge and able to look up and down the Chesapeake Bay. It was a clear day and many sails dotted the water.

"I've gotten to be a right good sailor," Jaime said proudly. "Now in the summer I'm going on a naval ship for three months. I doubt if I'll have time to come to Yuma. I sure would like to see Grandma Albright again. I saw her all alone for a whole afternoon before I had to report to the Academy."

"I don't know if I'll settle in Yuma," Lorraine said. "I now have the opportunity to look at the whole country and I might just find another place I want to live. I do have a job skill and can earn a living."

"What is that?"

"I'm an auto mechanic. And a good one too."

"Cool, Mom I'm proud of you." Jaime said just as they got off the bridge.

Lorraine pulled her motorhome into a restaurant parking lot. She took a deep breath and cried.

"Mom what's the matter?" Jaime asked anxiously.

"It's what you just said."

"What did I say to upset you?"

"Not upset, but you made me just so happy when you said 'Mom, I'm proud of you.' That is the most beautiful thing anyone ever said to me. Excuse me, but I just have to let these tears of joy out. Please bear with me."

"I mean it, Mom, you suffered greatly, really for no fault of your own, and you are coming out on top. You are a strong woman and I admire that."

"Jimmy, you are wise beyond your years."

"Mom, could I ask you something?"

"Sure,"

"Jimmy is a little boy. Please call me either Jim or Haime, whatever you prefer."

"You are my son. Just like I no longer want to be called Lori but Lorraine. Deal, Jim. Now one more thing I have to say to you. I have been wanting to tell you this for many years in person."

"Yeah, what's that?"

"I love you, Jim. Now are you ready to eat?"

"Always."

"Unless you are familiar with a good restaurant around here, how about this one?"

"Looks good, we can sit here and look at the water. Something I just can't get enough of."

"Who would have thought that a desert rat like you would go to the Naval Academy?"

"Life takes us on strange paths," Jaime said as they walked into the restaurant.

They sat on the patio overlooking the bay and slowly eating soft crabs with trimmings. They sipped on sodas and, after a while, ordered dessert. They enjoyed the strawberry short cake, the scenery, and the fact that they were together again.

Before darkness fell, they drove back to the Academy camp ground and both spent the night in the little Jamboree motorhome.

୧୬୧୬

The next morning over breakfast of bacon and eggs with bagels Jaime said, "Mom, if you don't have anywhere urgent to go, why don't you just hang around here for a little while. Next week is June week and there will be a lot of activities. You might enjoy seeing them."

"June week? But it's only May."

"It used to be in June."

"What will be going on?"

"So many activities, like graduation, for one. Of course, I'm not there yet. But the exciting thing the plebes do, is to place a hat on the Herndon Monument."

"Tell me about it."

"You see, the monument is this twenty-one foot

granite obelisk honoring a captain that went down with the ship off Cape Hatteras back in 1857. Someone puts a plebe Dixie cup on top and greases the whole monument with lard, I think. The plebe's job is to climb up, remove the Dixie cup, and replace it with an officer's hat. The legend is that the one who reaches the top is the first one from his class to become a flag officer."

"How long does that take?"

"The record is twenty minutes, but it can take as long as four hours. It's wild. All I've seen is videos of it. That's our initiation to become upper class-men."

"Sounds like something worth seeing. I think I'll stay."

"Great, Mom, but they tell me to get around town that day it's faster to walk than drive. I can get you maps of where all the events are, and the times, so for the most part, you'll have to be on your own. The Academy owns my body right now."

"I know what it's like to have an institution own your body."

"I'm sure you do," Jaime said, looking sad.

"Cheer up, Son. Now my body is my own. I have good walking shoes and strong legs. What are we going to do today?"

"They really expect me to go to church. How about you and I drive over to St. Mary's Catholic Church for mass?"

"That would be wonderful. What so many people

take for granted to me is now new and wonderful. I never thought life could ever be this good again."

"For me this is wonderful, too. I did not realize just how much I have been missing you. There was a time I had almost forgotten you. I never received any mail and was not allowed to send you any letters."

"I did write to you children to begin with, but was told you never received my letters and cards. Then I just figured that I'd save the money for postage. My mother and Frank were the only ones I had contact with."

"Some time in the future I would like for you to tell me what it is like in jail."

"It will be long time before I want to talk about that. It's getting late. We'd better get ready for church. You have to tell me how to get there, or should I program my GPS?"

"I know the way very well."

"That's good. I hope you always know the way."

ℰↄℰↄ

Annapolis was pulsing with excitement during June Week of 2016. Relatives had come in from all over the whole country to help the midshipmen celebrate gradua- tion. Lorraine sat in the warm sunshine near the chapel and watched as, every fifteen minutes, a newly married couple emerged from the chapel.

They passed through the arches of raised swords and

the last sword bearer would give the bride a whack on the backside.

"What is the significance of the bride having to get whacked?" She asked a young woman sitting next to her with a toddler.

"It's the initiation into being a Navy wife," said the young mother.

The next couple emerged and the bride did not get her back side slap. "That bride is lucky, she did not get hit," Lorraine commented to the mother.

"Most likely she too is a naval officer. It's an offense to hit an officer."

"Do you have any idea how many women go here?" Lorraine asked.

"It's about twenty percent."

"That many? Good for the girls."

Later that day, Jim met her and the two went to a concert given by the church choir.

"Mother, it has been wonderful having you here for the last ten days. I'm glad Grandparents Lopez did not come. I had told them I'd come for a visit when I get back from sea duty. At the moment, I don't know if that can happen. Sometimes ships get delayed, especially now a days with all the crap going on in the world. This is the last day we can spend together 'cause tomorrow I'll be bussed to Norfolk to get on a ship."

"What kind of ship will you be serving on?"

"An LST, that means Landing Ship Tank."

"That means nothing to me," Lorraine said with a sigh. "Now I have to study about naval ships and protocol and all that. I'll soon be an officer's mother. Son, I'm proud of you."

"Where are you going next, Mom?"

"I was figuring I'd just head north. I want to visit New England and hopefully, just little towns. Big cities and all that traffic is really not my cup of tea. I'll visit state and national parks. Being in nature rejuvenates me. I seem to draw energy from being among trees and the water. Cities seem to sap my energy."

"I know what you mean. I draw energy from the ocean or the water going into the ocean. I'll write to Grandma Albright. When you get back to Yuma, you can see where I've been."

"And I'll send you postcards along the way. Good bye, my son."

Since they were in the privacy of the motorhome, she felt at liberty to give Jaime a lengthy hug. After he kissed her on the cheeks, he left the vehicle and walked back to the dormitory. Lorraine watched him go with straight back and his head held high.

"Dad, are you watching your grandson? I'm sure you too are very proud of him."

Chapter 15

Rejuvenated and feeling joyfully alive, Lorraine unplugged her rig and headed into the unknown. At first her course was west, until she found a scenic small road that headed north. Her first stop after Annapolis was the Gettysburg Battle Field. As she toured the historic site, she felt the pain and turmoil the soldiers must have felt over 150 years ago. She wondered how many ghosts of young lives lost still haunted the place. That evening, she went into her rig, ate a light meal, and cried. She cried for all the pains of the past.

After a while she told herself, "That is enough now. Tomorrow I'll go to a happier place."

She traveled through central Pennsylvania, enjoying the green countryside with well-kept farms. She was used

to seeing the bare rocky hills around Yuma. Here, the
hills were green with trees. Occasionally, she would meet
and pass a black buggy pulled by a horse. She waved to
the Amish in the buggy and they returned her greetings.

She stopped at a rest stop. With the good bread she
had bought at a small town bakery and the lunch meat
from a butcher shop she made herself a delicious sandwich. Sitting at a picnic table, she relished the meal. Then
she heard someone whining behind her. Glancing down,
she saw a dirty white puppy that looked in dire need of
food. The little animal looked at her with big, beady
black eyes and a hopeful expression. Its tail, with long
matted hair, waved at her, trying desperately to be noticed. Lorraine looked around. There was no one else at
the rest stop. Nearby was rolling farm land.

"Hello, little fellow. I suppose you're hungry."

She gave him some bread with butter on it and some
ham. The little critter ate it quickly and stared at her, hoping for more. She gave him some more, got a bowl, and
filled it with water. The animal lapped it up then looked
at her with pleading eyes.

"Well, little fellow, it looks like you need me. God
knows I need you. I didn't know that five minutes ago,
but now I do. Tell you what I'll do. In the next town I'll
buy you some dog food and a leash and some toys. Then
we'll find you a groomer and a vet. I'll have you checked
out and vaccinated. If everything is good, you and I will
be a family. Do you think you'll like living in a mo-

torhome and traveling? I think right now you would be happy to live in a card board box just as long as you get fed. Come, little fellow, we have things to do this afternoon."

In Wilkes Barre, she found a pet store where she could get the dog groomed.

"We have an opening right now," said the girl at the counter. "Just leave the dog with me and you can come and get him in about an hour and a half. What is the dog's name?"

"I haven't named him yet, just found him at the rest stop some miles back. Hmm, if it is a he, I'll call him Sami. What breed would you say this dog is?"

"I would guess that dog is a mix of poodle and Shih Tzu. Yes, it is a he."

"Do you know any vets around here?"

"Yes, there is one just a few doors away. I suggest you make an appointment while he's being groomed."

"I'll do that, then I get some supplies I need for him. I'll be in the store when he's finished."

"Good. I'll find you then." The girl took the dog and went back to the grooming area with him. "Come, Sami, you are going to be such a pretty boy when I get done with you,"

Lorraine's shopping cart was overflowing with supplies. There were several dozen cans of dog food, some dry dog food, snacks, a rawhide bone to cut his teeth on, bowls, a rack to put the bowls in, and an assortment of toys. "I see you have a lucky dog," said the elderly lady working as a cashier. "He should be happy playing with all those pretty toys. I haven't seen you before here, are you new in town?"

"No, I'm just passing through."

"And you are traveling with your dog? How does he like that?"

"He'll have to get used to it."

Just then the groomer came up, carrying a beautiful little white dog with a blue bow on the curly hair on top of his head.

"Here is your little Sami now," said the girl, handing over the dog.

"This is Sami? I can't believe it. He is beautiful. Does not look like the same dog at all."

"Yes, I cut a lot of matted hair off. Since it's summertime, his body feels good with short hair."

"I'm glad you left it long on the tail. That looks like he is waving a white flag. Thank you so much."

Lorraine slipped an extra five dollars in the girl's pocket. She gave the cashier the money for the grooming. She put a harness and leash on the dog and carried her bag of supplies to the motorhome. Then she walked him to the veterinary hospital.

"Little Sami is a healthy little dog, I'll just give him his puppy shots," the young vet said. "Where did you get him?"

"I found him, or rather he found me when I stopped

for lunch at a rest stop. He was a real mess before he was groomed."

"So the poor critter has been dumped," he said. "No telling how long he's been there. I think that's disgusting when people dump little animals like that. I would like to get a hold of one of those dumpers and I wouldn't be nice to them. More people should get their animals spayed or neutered. In about two to three months, you should get him fixed."

"I'm traveling in my motorhome. I don't know where I'll be in three months."

"That's great. Someday I'll do that. But first I have to work and pay off my student loans. Where are you off to after beautiful, wonderful Wilkes Barre?

"I want to go to New England and who knows where?"

"Lady, I envy you. Do you work along the way?"

"I have been known to do that. For some reason, people find me if their car needs fixing."

"You're a mechanic. Tell you what I'll do. My car is sitting out back and I've been having some real problems with the old clunker. If you could take a look at it, I can do some adjusting on the vet bill."

"Sounds good to me. Can I pull my rig around back near your car? I have a bunch of tools in my storage compartment."

Lorraine parked next to the young doctor's car and gave him a tune up.

He came out, tested it, and was pleased with the healthy sound of the engine.

"I had to buy some spark plugs," she said. "I estimate the job to be worth a hundred bucks."

"That is just what my bill would have been."

The doctor extended his hand and wished her a good journey. Lorraine took Sami for a walk and was happy to see him relieve himself. She put him in the motorhome where he promptly peed on the floor.

"I suppose you want to mark it as your possession. Just don't do it again."

Just outside of town, she found a nice camp ground where she paid to spend one night. While walking the dog, more people stopped to talk to her and admire the cute little animal. Soon the conversations were dogs, dogs, and more dogs, spiced with someone telling her about their cat.

This was the first time she'd ever had a dog. Now she realized that she had been missing a lot.

That night when she went to bed, she had a warm loving body next to her. It had been over fifteen years since there had been anything else in her bed. She reached down and felt his soft fur. Then she felt a soft warm tongue licking her hand. She fell asleep with a contented smile on her face.

Having a dog in her life changed her routine. No more sitting in quiet meditation while having her morning coffee, now she took the dog for a walk. She carried a plastic bag to pick up his droppings. The dog enjoyed having a ball tossed and he would return it to her. When she was happy, the dog smiled, when she felt sad, the dog snuggled up to her as if to say, "It will be all right, don't be sad."

Soon she loved the little creature so much that she hadn't known she could love that much again.

Lorraine had built a wall of defense around her emotions. She felt she had been hurt more than any human being could take. First to be so disappointed by Alexandro. Then loving her babies and suddenly not having any contact with them while she was imprisoned for self-defense.

At first her heart ached more than she could stand, but slowly a scab built around it. When she was at the college trying to contact daughter Rachel she was not surprised to get a definite rejection and be referred to as *that* woman.

She wondered if all the negativity the girl had heard about her all those years would ever be replaced by an agreement to see her. Then there was Jaime, her wonderful beautiful son Jaime. The one she could connect with and who accepted her and even expressed that he was proud of her. That warm feeling restored some of her happiness. Now she felt hope that it could happen with the girls.

I just have to give them time, she told herself. *Maybe Maria will go away to college and I will go see her there.*

One thing I'm still afraid of. I do not want to go to the Lopez house in Yuma.

One night she was in a campground in Vermont. It was in the middle of the week and the heavily wooded camp ground was almost empty.

The lady in a nearby space invited Lorraine in. "I have been fishing, and I have more fish than I need. Would you like to join me for supper?"

"I would love it. May I bring some beer or wine?"

"Sure, that will go good with the trout."

"Beer or wine?"

"Why not both?"

"You got it."

The two women sat around the campfire until past midnight, talking. The conversation started with the fisherman, named Pam, showing her lures which she had made herself and proudly displayed. Then they went into girl talk. Lorraine, who was feeling the effect of the wine, did not hold back and told about her life.

Pam was not shocked that she was having a meal with an ex-con. "It seems to me you were railroaded. Now if I were you, I would never want to live in Yuma again. You now have a good trade. You could work anywhere. I wish there was a good mechanic in my town in New Hampshire. Why don't you come and live there?"

"Does it snow a lot there?"

"There is more snow than you have ever seen."

"Would you believe it? This coming September I'll

be thirty-eight and I have never seen snow up close. I have never felt snow on my face or in my hands. I do want to experience snow, but I don't like the cold. Thank you for the invite to live in your town, but I will settle in a warmer place. Maybe on the outskirts of Phoenix. I have a brother and his family there, and maybe my mother would like to find an apartment there, too."

"Don't you want to live with your mother?"

"If I live with her, she'll impose all kinds of rules as if I was fifteen. No, for the first time in my life, I want to be on my own. I have my little lover right here," Lorraine said, pointing to Sami who was laying at her feet looking at the fire.

"That sure is a cute dog. Those Shih Tzus are smart dogs, you picked well."

"He picked me."

"God knew you needed him, that's why you found him. There are times I say to God, 'Father there is something or someone I need in my life, please bring it to me.' Just today I looked at my fish and thought, I really don't want to eat alone tonight, and just then you pulled your rig in."

"I have never been told that I was an answer to a prayer. Thank you."

"I'm glad you got to know your son and now have a relationship with him. Eventually your girls will realize their mother is an amazing woman."

"Pam, it sure was a pleasure meeting you and spending the evening with you."

"You got plans for tomorrow? Like, do you have to go on or would you like to spend the day with me and I can teach you to fish?"

"No, there is no one expecting me. Another day in this beautiful God's country would be nice. What do you say, Sami, do you want to stay another day here?" The dog gave one bark. "I suppose that was a yes. Okay Pam, I'll stay."

The two women enjoyed the day together and caught a sufficient amount of fish for supper. Pam showed her how to release a fish, causing as little harm as possible. "I only take what I use," she said. "I hate those fishermen who see how many fish they can get and brag about it and then waste them."

"Yes," Lorraine said, "there are people that worship a God they cannot see, but trample on nature they can see."

"You're right. I believe that God is everywhere, in all nature in all animals, just everywhere. I don't need to go into a building to worship."

Lorraine said nothing, talking about religion made her uncomfortable.

Early next morning, the two newly found friends exchanged phone numbers and gave each other a warm hug. Pam stood with her fishing rod in her hand as she waved good-bye to Lorraine.

Chapter 16

Driving along in Vermont, Lorraine passed a small airport. A big sign advertising glider rides caught her attention. She turned in and inquired about it.

"Yeah, I can take you for a glider ride today. I can take you up in about an hour."

"Great, how much is it?"

"That's $120.00 for an hour."

"You have a deal."

An hour later, Lorraine sat in the glider being towed up by a small plane. Then the rope was released and they were sailing through the air. The pilot sat in the back.

Lorraine expected a glider to be silent, but the air going through it made noise. They went high into the air and she laughed with excitement. "Can you make a loop?" she asked the pilot.

"No, we don't make loops."

"Too bad."

The hour ended all too soon and the pilot had to force the plane down for a landing.

Eventually, they landed on the grassy field of the little airport.

"That was the biggest thrill I've had in a long time," she exclaimed.

"Have you ever been up in a balloon?" the pilot asked.

"No, I never have."

"When you get to Burlington, see my friend and go for a balloon ride."

"Thanks, I hope I can afford it. The way I've been spending money, I'm running low. Are there any jobs around here?"

"What can you do?"

"I'm a certified auto mechanic."

"Great. I could use your help right here at the airport. Our truck here needs some work. When can you do it?"

"Right now. Anyplace I can park my rig?"

"You can park it near the office there. We can provide electric and water. To dump you have to go somewhere else."

"I'm good in that department. I can go a good week."

"How much you charge for your mechanic work?"

"I'll just take what you give me when the job is done. I know you'll be fair."

"You got a deal."

For the next week, Lorraine put in five-hour work days, fixing a truck and checking out some of the cars of the people that worked at the airport. Soon friends of theirs came with their old rusty cars and Lorraine got their engines humming like a well-tuned cello. One of the pilots brought his little dog to work and kept him in a fenced in area. When Sami was put in the enclosure, the two dogs became friends right away and played together. Sami was happy, the other little dog was happy, therefore Lorraine was happy.

Everyone at the airport appreciated her mechanical skill and extended New England hospitality by inviting her to their houses for supper. At the end of the week, Lorraine had received enough money to get her quite a ways down the road. She bid everyone a warm farewell, got back into her rig, and drove off. Sami seemed sad at first at leaving his friend.

"I'm sorry, little fellow, but there is too much to see in the USA to remain in one place. We have a lot more states to visit before winter sets in. You and I don't want to drive in snow and ice."

They drove along in the lovely countryside and Lorraine was singing.

She found the balloon rides in Vermont quite pricey and decided to put that adventure off for another place and time. Then she drove over to Maine and followed the ocean front highway north. It went through small towns that were the support of boats and yachts. In Bar Harbor, a lobster man took people out in his boat for a fee. About a dozen people went with him. The man was a real teacher and, within an hour or two, not only could every one enjoy being out on a boat, but one got a lesson in lobstering.

Lorraine learned that any lobster not weighing between one pound and a quarter to one pound and a half was not a Maine lobster. He also said that if a lobster had eggs on her, the tail was nicked and, henceforth, she was immune from ever being caught again. Of all the lobsters pulled up in the trap, most of them were again released, either due to size or the mark of immunity. Lorraine was happy that lobstering was done with so much attention to conservation. After she got off the boat, she went to a restaurant for lunch and enjoyed a delicious steamed lobster. A lobster, fresh off the boat was something one did not experience in Yuma.

That afternoon, she again went into a campground. It was the Quoddy Head State Park. And again she was invited to share a fire and some fish. But this time it was by a man.

Lorraine was walking Sami on a path overlooking the Atlantic Ocean. She sat down at a point of land and just inhaled the view. Along came a hiker and sat near her to do the same. He was about six feet tall, his short medium brown hair was graying at the temples, and to make up for the loss of hair on his cranium he had a well-kept goatee. *He looks like a teacher, maybe a college professor. I suppose he is just a two or three years older than me.*

"Do you realize this is the eastern most point of land in the United States?" he asked.

"Yes, I read that in the brochure they gave me when I came in."

"I plan to be here when the sun rises and be among the first people in the country to see the new day. What brings you to this part of the country?"

"Simply the fact that I have never been here before."

"Where are you from, if I may ask?"

"Yuma, Arizona. And you?"

"Albuquerque."

"Oh really, and what brings you here?"

"Because I have never been here before."

"Are you on vacation?" she asked.

"I call it a working holiday."

"Oh, what kind of work do you do? If I'm not too prying."

"I'm a painter of pictures, or to be more elegant, an artist."

"Oh how interesting. May I see what you have painted?"

He pulled some up on his camera and showed them to her. "Here are some of the pictures I have painted."

"They are lovely landscapes, and so diversified. Your water looks like one could dive into it. Are any of your pictures for sale?"

"For a price, they all are for sale."

"I have a spot in my motorhome that could use a small painting. Do you have anything no larger than about twelve inches and not too expensive?"

"I might have a water color that would fit the bill. What do you call not too expensive?"

"The max I can afford is a hundred dollars."

"We can talk about it. I did some fishing today and caught a nice flounder. It's really too big for one person. Would you do me the honor of helping me eat it? While you are there, I can show you the water colors I have aboard."

"Thank you, that would be great. What space are you at?"

"I'm at number eighteen."

"My lucky number, eighteen is my birthday.

"Oh, really, what month?"

"September."

"What a coincidence, I have a birthday too."

"What, September eighteenth?"

"No, November twenty-second."

"Where is the coincidence?"

"I said that I have a birthday, not on the same day."

"Oh, I see. You're a joker." She laughed. "What time do you want me to show up for supper?"

"How would six o'clock be?"

"Good, I'll be there. I better get back now, time to feed Sami."

"That sure is a cute little dog."

"I'll just leave Sami at home when I come. By the way, you have not told me your name."

"And you haven't told me yours. I'm Guy Walcott."

"And I'm Lorraine Lopez."

"Nice meeting you, Miss Lopez."

"Please, Lorraine will do."

"And Guy is enough for me. See you later, Lorraine."

At six Lorraine knocked on the body of a class-A motorhome.

"Come aboard," Guy said, taking her hand and leading her up the steps.

"Nice rig. You must do well as an artist."

"I make a living. Now what would you like to drink? Anything with a little kick?"

"Just a little kick, got any beer?"

"Two beers coming up," he said, reaching into the refrigerator. "Now tell me about yourself."

"There really is not much to tell. I have been living in Arizona all my life and now I'm seeing the country."

She studied the tall man with the intense green eyes. His physique looked like he was used to working out. She wondered if her body measured up to his standards. When she got out of jail, she was a bit on the plump side, but lately she noticed her clothes getting quite loose on her. His looks appealed to her. She wondered if she appealed to him.

Lorraine sat in the settee, watching him prepare the fish. He put it in a pan, spread butter and lemon juice on top, then sprinkled on salt and pepper. The oven was already hot when he put in the fish.

"I hope you like baked sweet potatoes."

"Love them."

"I have some plain yogurt we can put on them, if you like."

"Thank you, I think I'd like mine plain."

While they were eating at the big window overlooking the ocean, Lorraine kept Guy talking about himself. Whenever he asked her a question about her life she gave a brief non-committal reply and asked him more about himself and his art. He mentioned that he'd had showings at some renowned galleries in some big cities.

"Where are you going from here," she asked.

"I want to head up to Nova Scotia. Why don't you go there too? If you are the least interested in maritime history, that might be an interesting place to go."

"I never thought much about ships and the sea, but now I have a son in the Naval Academy and I find it fascinating. Only thing is, I can't go tomorrow. I have a reservation to go out on a schooner for a sail for tomorrow. I have already paid for it, no refund unless they cancel."

"Then you better go, you'll like it. Could I have your

phone number and I'll call you. Maybe we can meet in Nova Scotia. That would be nice."

"The boat ride is only for half a day. Can you wait for me and we can have our two rigs travel together?"

"That's an option. I could take a lot more pictures here and I can always do a little painting. Are you still interested in a picture?"

"Most definitely."

"I have one you might especially be interested in."

He showed her a picture of Quoddy Head. The back of a woman with a small white dog were in the picture. The woman was overlooking Quoddy Narrows.

"Did you just paint that picture today?"

"Yes, you like it?"

"It's fantastic. How much do you want for it.?"

"Your undying love and gratitude."

"I don't know if I can afford that."

"How about a peck on the cheek then?"

"That I can afford." She gave him a little kiss on the cheek.

"That was a down payment. Another kiss on the other cheek will pay it off in full."

She gave him a kiss on his left cheek. Then he put his arms around her and gave her a kiss on the lips. When they broke apart he said, "Now there, you have just paid for another painting."

"Thank you so much for the delicious dinner and the painting, but I better go and take Sami for a walk. Then I hope to get reception 'cause I need to call my mother in Yuma. Last time I talked with her she was not feeling well. Thank you again, and good bye."

Quickly she left the motorhome and went into hers. Sami was eagerly awaiting her and his walk.

I have been kissed by a man. Wow, it has been over fifteen years since I have been really kissed by a man. It felt good. I like it. Maybe I shouldn't have rushed away. Maybe I should go back and see where it goes. Forget it, girlfriend, you have never been a slut. You're not going to start now.

You have killed a man, but you are no slut. I wonder how he would feel if he knew everything about me. I feel like I'm dragging a big trunk of secrets. I told Pam about my background and she was not shocked nor did she seem to be afraid of me after that. Anyway, I have to play it cool to whom I tell. Just enjoy the moment and remain a little mysterious.

She called her mother while walking the dog.

"Hello, Lori, good to finally hear from you."

"Yes Mom, sorry it has been a few days, but sometimes there just was no reception. How are you feeling?"

"I still don't feel up to par, and now I have a contract on the house. Where are you, Lori?"

"I'm about as far away from Yuma as I can get and still be in the United States. I'm in eastern Maine."

"Lori, I hate to be a bother to you, but I need to move and I really could use your help."

"Where are you planning on moving to?'

"Frank convinced me that I should move to Phoenix and be near them. At least I have two grandsons there. In the fall, Maria will go to college in Flagstaff. Then I'll have no grandchildren here anymore. Other than my friends, there is really nothing to keep me in Yuma."

"I'm glad to hear that, Mom. I was hoping you'd move out of Yuma. I certainly don't want to live there anymore. One of the Lopezes might see to it that I have a fatal accident. I certainly wouldn't put it past them."

"Oh, Lori, don't say that. I'm sure they wouldn't harm you. Now how soon can you get here?"

"Gee, Mom, if I push it and just drive the fastest way, I'm sure it will be a good week to get to Yuma. And today I met someone who looks interesting."

"Well, then you better just stay there and get a little piece and forget about me here all by myself, needing your help."

"No Mom, don't take it like that. I'm not here to get 'a little piece.' He seems like a very nice gentleman. He had invited me to dinner in his motorhome and gave me a water color he did. I'll take off and return to Yuma. But like I said, it's going to take a good week for me to get there. I hope you sort things out you don't want to take, and we might be able to do a garage sale."

"Good idea. I'll do that. It will be a few months before the sale will be final. Good bye, I'm glad you finally called."

"You know, Mom, you can call me too. I have the phone off when I'm driving, but you can leave a message."

"It has been so long since I was able to call you, I just forgot that I can."

Lorraine went to Guy's rig and knocked. He was wearing a silk robe when he answered the door. "Oh, what a surprise. I hope you have good news."

"No, I spoke with my mother and she is not too well. Another thing, she has to move and has asked me to come back and help her. Immediately after the boat ride, I'll need to start for Yuma. I wish I could go to Nova Scotia with you, but I'm afraid that's out."

"I'm sorry to hear that. I will stay in touch with you, I promise."

"That would be nice. The good news is that she's planning on moving to Phoenix. I have a brother there. That is even closer to Albuquerque than Yuma."

"All I can say is *Que sera sera*. What will be will be."

"You're not old enough to remember that song."

"Neither are you."

The morning was still very cool when Lorraine took Sami for a walk. Guy was wearing his hiking clothes and walked with her. "Do you have any idea how you will travel?" he asked her.

"I plan to cut across New York to Buffalo. I do really want to stop and visit Niagara Falls, then head west, cutting through Ontario to Detroit, and then around lake Michigan on the southern end going west on the northern roads. Eventually, I'll head south to Yuma."

"You better warn your mother that it will be at least ten days on the road."

"Yes, ten days of hard driving. Thank you, Guy, for walking with me. I better catch that boat and then I have many roads to travel before I can rest."

"Yes, parting is such sweet sorrow."

"Romeo and Juliet," she exclaimed, surprised.

"Ah, you know Shakespeare."

"Yes, I found that one has to read Shakespeare with leisure and deep concentration, then one finds the pearls."

"I wish we had more time, but I must bid you fare thee well."

She gave him a brief kiss on his lips, quickly got into her motorhome, and drove off.

I wish I could just stay, darn. Guy looks like an interesting fellow and I wish we could have gotten acquainted better. Is there a man out there I could have a relationship with? Would I be able to give myself to a loving relationship? I suppose I can. Jaime was the first to crack my wall of defense. I love that young man. Then Sami showed me that I can love.

Do I go to my mother as a dutiful daughter or is it love? Am I responsible for her welfare? She only visited me in prison not even ten times in those fifteen years. Frank, bless his heart, was the only one who was loyal and came every other month or so. Enough of these pathetic thoughts. Now I'm going to enjoy the boat ride on the schooner and then, next stop, Niagara Falls.

Chapter 17

Two days later, Lorraine stopped at a camp ground near Niagara Falls. She plugged in, hooked up the water and sewer, and took Sami for a walk. Other rigs pulled in and did the same. She concentrated on the little dog, and picking up his droppings, and paid no attention to a motorhome with a New Mexico license plate. She heard her name being called. She looked around and there was Guy walking up behind her at a brisk pace. "Guy, what are you doing here?"

"I'm waiting for a certain gal from Yuma. You look just like her. Have you seen her by any chance? She has a little dog that looks like that dog's brother."

"Oh, Guy," she said, entering his embrace. "How good to see you. I thought you were going to Nova Scotia."

"I thought so too, but the motorhome got lost and found its way to Niagara Falls."

"What a pleasant surprise. It's good to see you. Catch any more fish?"

"No, I haven't been fishing. But I got some good sausages at a butcher shop. Would you do the honor of joining me for supper?"

"When did you get here? I didn't see you pass me on the road."

"I arrived an hour ago," he said. "Where did you stop last night?"

"I stopped near Montpelier, Vermont.

"I went a bit farther yesterday. If you are free tomorrow, would you want to go on a boat ride with me?"

"I'd love that," she said.

"Good. I already bought two tickets for tomorrow on the *Maid of the Mist*. So then we have a date."

"We have a date."

Gosh, we have a date. A real date to go out on a boat. He has no idea what that means to me. Now we'll have supper together and who knows where that will lead? Yippee, I'm so excited. Keep calm, kid, don't really show how you feel. Just stay cool, that way he thinks he is making a conquest. I might as well enjoy it as long as it lasts. When I tell him the truth about myself, that will most likely be the end of it. Enjoy the moment as it comes.

Guy had a motor scooter in the basement of his rig. They needed motorized transportation to get from the campground to the falls. They both got on the scooter and rode on the road. He parked it and they walked along the falls on a sidewalk with a railing.

"Aren't these the most magnificent sights you have ever seen?" Lorraine asked Guy.

"One of the world's top magnificent natural wonders." Guy said, getting photos from every angle. Then he took a picture of Lorraine.

"Please, don't take a picture of me. I don't even have any lipstick on and my hair is a mess, I'm sure."

"You don't need paint to be beautiful, let me use the paint. I like your natural look."

"Oh Guy, you are such a flatterer."

"It's not flattery, I mean it."

"Thank you," she said softly, looking down.

They sat on a bench and watched the falls change colors in the fading light.

"I would love sitting here until it's completely dark, but I don't like riding the scooter at night. We better get back to the camp ground."

Guy took the handle bars and controls and Lorraine sat on the long seat, holding on with her arms around his waist. She enjoyed having such close contact with a man. He dropped her off at her rig and wished her a good night. Then he proceeded to his larger class-A and turned in there.

I wonder. I wonder if he can still function in the sex department, or if he is inclined to function that way.

When I was seventeen, the first thing boys wanted was to jump into my pants. Now Guy is such a sexy looking man, but he has not made a single move in that direction. Are there really gentlemen left who don't try to seduce a gal right off the bat? Tomorrow we go for a boat ride, then I better invite him for lunch. What can I make? Will Oodles of noodles and some spam do? That is about all I can think of to offer. No, a better idea would be to invite him out to lunch in a nice restaurant overlooking a beautiful view. I suppose we'll have to pay for the view with our lunch. Gal, stop worrying, just play it by ear tomorrow.

Lorraine went to bed. "Come, Sami, time to go to sleep. Come to Mommy."

The dog jumped up on bed, snuggled up to her chest, and gave her a gentle lick on the chin.

"Good boy, Sami, good night."

ဇာဇာ

The boat ride on the *Maid of the Mist* was thrilling beyond words. Everyone received a raincoat with a hood before boarding the boat. As the boat approached the falls, the mist fell like heavy rain.

Lorraine took off the rain coat and let the water flow over her while she laughed. "This is wonderful, simply wonderful."

"You're getting soaking wet."

"So what? The day's warm and I'll dry off. I want to

experience Niagara Falls falling over me. Hallelujah, this is wonderful."

After they disembarked the boat, they sat on a bench in the sunshine and dried off. Guy too, had been showered by the falls.

"Thank you for this thrilling boat ride. Gosh, Guy, I'm so glad you are here with me. A joy shared is double the joy."

"And a pain shared is half the pain. I hope we get to share many joys," he said, looking into her eyes with a serious expression.

Can he really mean that? We only met a few days ago, we walked together, we ate two meals together, we had a glass of wine together. He can't seriously be interested in a relationship, not this early in the game. I know, the next thing, he'll ask to get in my pants. Well, mister, you're going to be disappointed. This time, I'm not going to be a push over for the first guy that flatters me. That did not stand me well the last time. And I had a long time to think about my mistakes.

"We're just about dry. Getting hungry?" he asked.

"Yes, a bit. Boat rides make me hungry."

"Me, too. I hear there is a good restaurant not far from here. We could walk there."

"I worry that a restaurant that close to the falls is really expensive. Maybe we could ride the scooter to another restaurant."

"This is the first time I'm here," he said. "I'm going

to live it up and go to the eatery close to the falls. You, my dear, are my invited guest. I'm just glad I'm not in this romantic spot by myself.

Oh, oh, here comes, a proposition.

"I think you misunderstand me," she said, "It's not that I can't afford to eat in an expensive place, it's just that I'm frugal and don't want to spend that much."

"I like frugal, but sometimes you just have to let go and circulate the money."

They went and ate at the overpriced restaurant, enjoyed an overpriced glass of wine, and relished the view. Lorraine was anxious to get back to the motorhome before Sami had an accident on the floor. They rode back and, to Lorraine's relief, Sami had been a good boy and didn't leave anything on the floor.

"You know, Guy, if you really want to see the complete sunset over the falls, we could just take my rig and drive over there. That way we don't need to travel back on the scooter."

"Isn't that a lot of trouble for you unhooking everything?"

"No big deal. I have to do it in the morning, anyway. I'll just do it tonight, and when we get back, only plug in the electric. Now, in the morning, I really do have to get underway toward Yuma. So let's drive back to the falls so you can get your artist's view of the sunset, and I hope it's a good one. I'm sure Sami will enjoy the walk along the falls again."

The sunset was not disappointing and, as the colors changed, Guy named the paints he would mix to get the right shade. They sat on the bench, Sami at her feet and Guy's arm over her shoulder.

Lorraine felt such contentment and belonging that she had forgotten even existed. A handsome man who said he cared for her by her side, and a loving pet at her feet, gave her a feeling of being needed. It was dark when they pulled the rig back into the campground.

Between the spaces was a wild area with tall grasses and daisies. Guy cut a tall, thin bouquet and gave it to her. She took it into the motorhome, found an empty beer bottle, put in the flowers and grass, added water, and put it into a cup holder on the settee table.

"There, that will remind me of you," she said.

"And what will you give me as a reminder of you?"

"I don't know. You got any suggestions?"

"In times of old, a damsel would give her knight a piece of fabric."

Lorraine took a red head scarf, cut it in half, and gave it to him with a kiss. "There, you have something to carry when you battle the highway. My mother is getting anxious for my return, so I better get back to Yuma the fastest way I can go."

"Then I hope you get a good night's sleep. I hope to see you off in the morning. I must say good night." He reached out, embraced her, gave her a tender kiss, and left the motorhome.

Good-bye, dear man. Most likely I will never see you again. Oh how I wish, I wish we could have been together longer. Maybe there could have been something developing between us two.

Lorraine went to bed and little Sami jumped up and took his place beside her.

"Oh Sami, can you tell me, is this possibly the real thing or are we just two ships passing in the night?" Sami licked her on the chin. "Is that a yes? Okay little fellow, one lick is a yes, two licks are a no."

Sami gave her three more licks.

"Now, is that an I don't know or a yes, yes, yes?"

Chapter 18

The light of day had barely started to illuminate the country side when Lorraine unplugged the electricity and took off. She was afraid if she enjoyed another embrace from Guy, she would never want to leave. *Whatever happens between the two of us is up to the fates. If we are meant for each other, no distance is too far. We will get together and share a life. It is in the hands of God.*

Suddenly, the road seemed very lonely. She was driving on the Ohio Turnpike doing sixty-five in a seventy mile an hour speed zone. Driving along on the right lane, keeping a safe distance from cars in front of her, she saw a police car hanging on her left. He just hung there. *Go around me. I don't like anyone hanging next to me. Sup-*

pose I have a blowout. The next thing she saw was a big flashing light on his roof. It scared the hell out of her. What could a cop possibly want? She signaled, pulled onto the shoulder, and stopped.

Quite a distance back she saw the police car and another car on the shoulder. *Oh, he stopped another car.* She signaled and, when it was safe, pulled back on the highway. Almost immediately two police cars were on her tail with lights flashing. Again, she signaled, pulled onto the shoulder, and stopped. Then she saw three police officers walk up beside her rig.

Keep calm, kid. You haven't done anything wrong. Stop shaking. She lowered the window of the passenger side.

A good looking young officer approached and said, "Good afternoon, ma'am, I just want to make sure you are okay."

Of course, I'm okay. Why?"

"I saw you weaving on and off the highway. I just want to make sure you're not sleepy. Are you alone?"

"No, I'm not alone, I have a dog." Just then Sami jumped up on the passenger seat. "If I was falling asleep, would I signal before I ran off the highway?"

"I suppose not. Do you have a driver's license, proof of insurance, and registration?"

Lorraine handed him all the required documents, which he took back to the police car. While he was gone, she looked around in her rig and suddenly it dawned on her why she was stopped. The police saw the beer bottle sitting in the cup holder from outside. She knew in many states there were laws about having open alcohol containers in a vehicle. They must not have seen the flowers stuck in the bottle from the outside of the motorhome.

When the officer returned, she said, "I suppose you thought there was a wild party going on in here."

"Yes, that's what it looks like from the outside. Everything is in order," he said, handing back her documents, "Have a good trip."

"Thank you."

Before she took off, she wrapped a paper towel around the beer bottle, took a deep sigh of relief, and continued on the highway.

That evening when she was in a campground for the night, she received a phone call from Guy. She told him about the attention she received with the beer bottle. He laughed. He told her that he would be visiting friends in Wisconsin. Then the phone faded and the last thing she heard was that he'd stay in touch.

She traveled I-80 to Des Moines then headed southwest, traveling a small road in New Mexico. When she got into Deming, she went to the same campground as before. But now most of the people were gone and there was no dance being held. Early the next morning she left, expecting to put in a 460 mile day before she reached her destination.

While driving on I-8 with very light traffic, she had

time to contemplate the trip. She had not done all she hoped to do. On the other hand, she could hope more good might come out of it yet.

Her stop at San Marcos was a failure. She really wanted to connect with her daughter. On the other hand, the stop in Annapolis was a roaring success. Briefly, she had taken time to do some sightseeing and enjoying the country side. Then she met Guy, a man she could not get out of her mind. She kept seeing his intense green eyes and hearing his calm masculine voice. She felt the warmth of his embrace, even though a week had passed since she'd felt it. She thought back with fondness at the wonderful time at Niagara Falls and wished it had been longer and possibly more intense. She felt a desire stirring in the pit of her stomach that she had almost forgotten. Having lived without sex for so long almost put that desire to sleep. Now she felt a want.

The other thing she needed to do was connect with her younger daughter. She did not know how she would do that. The only thing she could do would be to keep her eyes and ears open for an opportunity.

I'll get my chance. God wills it, I will get my chance. Hopefully, before too long, Rachel will come around and realize I'm not the ogre she was led to believe. Right now my biggest hope and desire is to re-connect with all three of my children. Please help me do that, dear Lord and Jesus and Holy Mary.

It was dusk when she finally pulled up in front of her

mother's house. Mary Albright rushed out of the house before Lorraine had pulled the parking brake on and extracted her body from behind the wheel.

"My dear girl, you finally are back," Mary said, giving her daughter a tight squeeze. "I'm so happy to see you. Been expecting you for the last five days."

"Good to see you too, Mom, but I told you it would be about ten days, and here I am. Ten days exactly. This is a big country."

"But you did not call me for five days and I left messages."

"There were times I was out of cell range. Main thing is, I'm here now."

"Not a moment too soon. I have to be out of the house in another week."

"Mom, before I do anything, I just have to get a bite to eat." She heard a bark from the motorhome. "Yes, I have a new member of the family to introduce you to. Mom, meet Sami," she said as she lifted the little dog out of the vehicle.

"Oh, what a cute little dog, but you can't bring him into the house. You know I'm allergic to dogs and cats."

"If you don't mind, I'll just stay in the rig and park her in the back yard. Hopefully, you can spare me an extension cord to plug in."

"No problem, I have a heavy duty cord so you can run the air conditioning."

"Great. First let me get a sandwich then I'll park her behind the house."

That done, and having taken Sami for a walk, she put him back into the little rig and went into her mother's house.

"Now tell me, what have you done and what do you still have to do to move?"

"I have secured an apartment in a senior complex in Phoenix. It's not too far from Frank. I have decided which furniture I'll take and what I'll get rid of."

"Have you tried selling any?"

"Put an ad in the paper, but haven't had much response."

"Maybe it would just be easiest to call the Salvation Army and have them come and get what you don't want." Lorraine looked around at her mother's old furniture and wondered if the Salvation Army would even be willing to take it. The couch had seen many years of bodies on it and showed it with sag marks. "Have you got a date with a moving company?"

"Not yet."

"If you need to be out of here in a week, you better call a moving company first thing in the morning. I'll help you pack your things and we'll get you moved to the big city. On the day of the closing on the house, we can drive over to Phoenix."

"Lori, I'm so glad you are here to help me out. I just found the whole process overwhelming. You have gotten to be quite a take-charge person. I wish I had your self-confidence."

"You'll be fine, Mom."

"I haven't even asked you how your trip went. Did you do what you hoped to do?"

"Yes and no. Rachel refused to see me, but I had a wonderful time with Jim, I told you that when I called."

"Yes, so you did," Mary said absently.

I wonder if Mom is getting senile. She seems to have problems remembering. I'll have to keep an eye on her. Maybe it's just a problem with hearing. Oh, God, I hope she's all right. I don't ever want to live with her again.

It ended up with Lorraine making all the moving arrangements. After having lived in Yuma most of her life, the July heat bothered Mary in a way her daughter had never seen before.

Mary would sit on the couch in the air-conditioned house with a cold glass of water and just say, "Lori, I have to rest. It's just too darn hot."

"Mom, how can you say it's too hot? It's only 109 and you are in a cool house."

"Maybe it's my age. I just can't take the heat like I used to."

"Mom, you're not that old. You're barely old enough for Medicare. Once this move is over and you're settled in, you'll feel better, I promise." *What a strange turn of events, I feel I'm talking to a child when I speak to my mother. She is acting like she is my child.*

"Yes, Mom," Mary said mockingly. "I'll get all the drawers in the bedroom packed today. Would you get the stuff in the kitchen?"

"All of it?"

"Yes, I'll take all of it."

"Are you sure you want to? The moving company charges by the pound."

"Well, maybe there are dishes I can give to Goodwill or the Salvation Army."

"Then you better sort out the kitchen, while I pack your clothes."

Mary did not do much sorting. At the end of the day, the items for disposal were very few and the boxes to go were heavy. While Mary was taking a nap, Lorraine went through the dishes, disposed of the chipped and cracked items, and quietly put them in the large garbage can outside.

"She'll never miss them and if she does, she'll yell at me."

When she rolled the large garbage can out to the curb for the pick-up, a black car with dark tinted windows slowly drove past the house. It almost came to a stop when it got near her. She could not see anyone inside.

Fear gripped Lorraine with a vengeance. She began to shake and break out in a cold sweat, in spite of the heat. Then the car slowly increased its speed and headed up the street. She didn't know why it frightened her so much. All she knew was that, suddenly, she received a signal of great danger. She was shaking when she went inside again. Mary was just coming out of the bedroom, still looking sleepy.

"I took a long nap. Did you get the kitchen all packed up?"

"Pretty much, Mom. You must have needed the sleep."

"Lori, I'm so glad you're here to help."

"Yes, Mom, me too." *She didn't even notice my shaking. Yuma is the last place in the world I want to be right now. Oh, Guy, come and rescue me.*

Lorraine had in her mind to go to her in-laws house and knock on the door, hoping her former mother-in-law would be reasonable and forgiving and let her see her daughter Maria. Now she dismissed that plan. Some people just had no forgiveness in their hearts. She remembered one of her prison friends telling her about her father-in-law. The man loved being angry at someone all the time. If he was not slighted, he imagined being slighted. The least little statement was twisted into the negative and never forgotten. As a matter of fact, in his mind, it was exaggerated and, when told to someone who did not know the original story, that person would think, *That poor man, why is everyone so mean to him?*

Lorraine went upstairs into her former bedroom and packed up to dispose of the things in that room. None of her things was still there, except some pictures on the walls she did not take with her when she got married.

Now she took them down to be disposed of. She stood near the window when the black car drove slowly by the house again.

This time she told her mother about the car. "Mom, there is a car that I saw driving by the house very slowly. It scared me."

"Lori, that's your imagination. What does the scary occupant look like?"

"I can't see anyone through the tinted windows."

"I see cars drive slowly all the time. The speed limit is twenty-five here. Some people even obey the law."

"Mom, I don't know why, but that car scares me. I would feel better if I take the rig and go to a gated RV park for the night. You can come with me."

"With the dog? You know I'm allergic to dogs."

"Mom, I'll just feel a lot safer away from here. I hope you won't mind."

"You go right ahead and go to a fancy park and maybe meet some fancy people and leave your old mother to handle everything alone."

"Mom, I'll be back in the morning and help you."

"Okay, I'll even come and get you and that way you can stay in the house and no one will know you're here."

"That sounds like a plan to me. I'll call you from a park when I get settled. I might as well go now. See you tomorrow then."

"Okay, Lori, see you then."

Driving toward the foothills, she stopped at an RV

park that had a flagpole near the gate with a huge American flag flying. There was no guard at the closed steel gate, but a call box. She pushed the button for the office and a friendly voice told her to come in. The gate opened.

Since it was July, there were many empty spaces, although over a hundred were occupied year round. "How long do you wish to stay?" asked the gray-haired lady at the reception desk.

"Maybe a week."

"If you pay for a week, it's cheaper than paying daily for five days."

"I'll pay for a week, how much?"

"One hundred twenty dollars."

Lorraine counted the money out. *I'm getting real low in funds now. As soon as the move is over, I hope to get a job in Phoenix.*

"Let me give you a receipt. What's your name?"

"Lorraine Albright."

"Very good, Miss Albright, and welcome to Sun Vista. We have both an indoor and outdoor pool. If you're interested, they will start playing volleyball in the indoor pool in an hour."

"That sounds like fun, thank you. I think I'll do that."

Lorraine parked her rig not far from the recreation complex. After taking Sami for a walk, she put on her bathing suit, covered it with a muumuu, and went to the pool house. After using the shower, she went to the pool where a number of people gave her a hearty welcome and invited her to play. "Come in, we need you," shouted a bald man. "That'll make an even six per side."

"Thank you, I'm coming."

She introduced herself with only her first name and everyone told her their first names.

"Enough social now, time to play ball," called the bald man.

Soon a beach ball was volleyed with passion. They played like the national honor hinged on the game. They played, everyone had fun, and no one kept score. After the game, the people wanted to get acquainted and shoot the breeze, but Lorraine excused herself, saying she needed to feed her dog.

"We hope you come back and play again," said one lady.

"I plan to, that was really fun."

Lorraine took a shower, washed her hair, and went back to her little motorhome where Sami gave her a warm welcome.

Chapter 19

The next morning, she stood at the front gate, for which she had received a clicker, and waited for her mother to come. Traffic on Thirty-Second Street was light, and she saw a black car with heavily tinted windows slowly drive past. Just then her mother arrived in her little silver Ford Focus. Quickly, Lorraine opened the gate and got in her mother's car. The gate was closing as her mother made a U-turn on the road.

"Lori, what's the matter you look pale and are shaking like a leaf."

"Mom, I saw the car that was driving by our house yesterday."

"Of all the cars in Yuma, how can you know it was the same car, and so what?"

"There are not that many black cars in Yuma, and I just have a real bad feeling about this particular car."

"You're silly. We need a lot to get done today."

Lorraine was hurt that her mother just poo-pooed her intuition. She just kept quiet and figured that in a few days this move would be over and she would be able to start a new life in Phoenix. The time could not go fast enough.

Her cell phone rang. She could see it was Guy. Suddenly, her mood improved.

"Hello, Guy," she answered.

"Lorraine, how are you?"

"I'm well, thank you. How's it going with you?"

"I'm stranded in Green Bay, Wisconsin. My transmission went out and it's in the shop being rebuilt."

"I'm sorry to hear that. I know that'll cost a pretty penny. Are you staying aboard?"

"No, the coach is in the garage and I'm staying with a friend."

A lady friend I assume. "I hope you get it repaired soon. Then where will you go?"

"I have a few art showings to do before I go back to Albuquerque. I'm getting tired of the travel. Now I realize that it just isn't all that much fun alone. How about you fly up here and travel with me?"

Get out of Yuma, travel in his nice thirty-two footer. That might just be the thing to do. Problem is, I don't have the money for the plane ticket. "Thank you, Guy.

That is a very tempting offer. I'll have to think about it and let you know. Right now, I have to get Mom moved, but that should be done in a few days."

"Don't think too long. I miss you."

"I miss you, too."

"Then there should not be too much to think about" he said.

"I'll let you know…" Then the call faded out.

"Who was that?" Mary asked.

"The very nice gentleman I met in Maine."

"Oh, what does he want?"

"He wants to meet me in Wisconsin and have me travel back with him."

Mary said nothing. Lorraine knew her mother did not like the phone call.

❦

That afternoon as Lorraine was putting trash in the big garbage can in front of the house, a black car came around the corner. She saw the tinted window was partially down and a round object was pointing in her direction. She dove behind the garbage can as she heard a loud bang. She felt the plastic garbage can give a jerk, then the car sped off. Lorraine thought her heart would jump out of her chest, it was beating so hard. Cautiously, she crawled out from behind the garbage can and looked. Sure enough, there was a little round hole in the can. She practically crawled back into the house and called the police.

Some of the officers who came were young and enthusiastic, others had been there over fifteen years earlier and were skeptical and calloused. Here was a woman who had killed her husband. Now someone was out to get her. Served her right, was their attitude. Two young cops searched the garbage can for the bullet. They found a .38 slug among the broken pottery and china.

That garbage saved her life. When Mary saw the dishes in the garbage, she did not scold her daughter for throwing them away. The next day the newspaper reported the shooting. The article surmised that it must have been a drug-related incident. After that, all the neighbors gave them nasty looks. When Mary and Lorraine drove up to her rig in the park they found a note at the door asking Lorraine to come to the office right away. She went with her mother and was told that she was no longer wanted in the park. She was to get her rig out immediately.

"Why?" she asked.

"We don't want your kind in our park," is all the woman said and turned her back.

Looks like it's no use asking for a refund for the days I'm not here. "Come, Mom, we don't want to be in a place like this, anyway."

"What are you going to do now, Lori?"

"I think you and I should just drive to Frank's and

not return until Saturday when the moving man comes. Fortunately, most everything is done, anyway. I'll call Frank and Kim and ask if it's okay to come. You can sleep in the house and I can just park on his driveway."

"Suppose the black car comes looking for us there. We'll put all of them in danger."

"Then if it makes you feel better, I'll take my coach and park her somewhere else."

"Oh Lori, Lori, Lori, what are we going to do?"

"We go on with our lives. What else can we do?"

"I think you should accept the invitation you got this morning."

"I think I'll call him and ask if it's still valid. Mom, I hate to ask you this, but could you lend me about five hundred dollars, no let me ask you for a thousand so I can pitch in for food with Guy."

"Since I'll be getting money in a few days, I can lend that to you."

"Thanks, Mom, I'll pay you back, that's for sure."

While Lorraine was walking Sami, she called Frank and told him her current situation.

"Sis, with you things are never dull. Of course, you are welcome here. We'll have the guest room ready for Mom when you get here."

Then she made one more call. "Guy, I have considered your offer, and I hope it's still valid."

"Of course it is. You mean you're coming?"

"Yes, as quickly as possible. I'll let you know when I book a flight."

"Good, I can't wait to see you."

Chapter 20

Guy was waiting in the airport with a big bouquet of colorful flowers. As she melted into his arms, Lorraine felt safe for the first time since she left him at Niagara Falls.

"Thank you for coming, sweets."

She just kept her face hidden in his sleeve. This moment was too sacred for words. It was not until this very moment that she realized just how much she loved the man.

I hope he loves me, too. I suppose he does, otherwise why would he ask me to come? Maybe he feels he wants a mechanic aboard. Did I ever tell him that I'm one? I don't remember.

"You hungry?" he asked. "I suppose you are since they don't feed you on the plane anymore. I know a good place for lunch. Is that all your baggage?" he said, looking at her small duffel bag.

"Yes, it is. For what the airlines charge for luggage nowadays, I can buy what I need at a thrift shop for less."

Guy laughed. "I like that you are thrifty. Then come, we can get out of here."

He led her to his motorhome parked at the airport. He put her duffel bag into the aft stateroom that contained a queen sized bed. "You can sleep here. I'll sleep on the couch in the other room."

"I hate to evict you from your bed. I'm happy to sleep on the couch."

"No, sometimes I get up in the middle of the night and make myself a cup of tea or chocolate. Then I look at my pictures and analyze them. I need the bright light I have there. You sleep in the bedroom and rest well."

He is so different from anyone I have ever known. Well, actually, I have not known many men. I got married when I was seventeen. I was faithful to my husband and then I lived in a nunnery for fifteen years. Now I wonder, is he is straight and what would he do if I told him where I spent fifteen years?

So many unanswered questions. I just have to play it cool and go with the program.

"I can tell from your face that this arrangement surprises you."

"Yes it does, but that is fine with me."

"I'm starving. Let's get some lunch and then, if

you're up to it, we'll take a little walk. What did you do with Sami?"

"He's at my brother's. His two sons just love him."

They went to a place that specialized in Italian cuisine. After lunch, they walked along Lake Michigan holding hands. Lorraine had so much to say, but was afraid to talk. They went for a boat ride on Lake Michigan aboard the *Foxy Lady*. Then they walked, mostly in silence, back to the motorhome.

"I have a gallery showing and reception in town here tonight. I hope you are free to come with me?"

"Let me check my calendar." She looked at the palm of her hand. "Yes, I can squeeze you in."

"Good, it starts at seven. Do you have a cocktail dress along or do you need to visit a thrift shop?"

"I brought something that should pass."

Guy was able to take the motorhome and park it across the street from the gallery. Lorraine spent the afternoon reading a book in the aft bedroom while guy was doing some watercolors. She took a shower and put on a red cocktail dress with hose and gold sandals with heels. A rhinestone clip sparkled in her short curled hair.

"Wow, you look terrific," Guy said with a whistle.

"Thank you, you look pretty decent yourself in your black tux."

"It is now ten after seven. Would you do me the honor of accompanying me to the gallery where they are ready to attack me?"

"Isn't attack a bit of a strong word?"

"You must never have been to an opening. You'll see."

When Guy and Lorraine walked in, people turned in their direction and clapped. Guy smiled and waved like a monarch. Lorraine just smiled. Someone handed each one of them a glass of champagne. Then people surrounded Guy and separated her from him. Lorraine walked around the gallery and looked at his paintings and watercolors. Some pictures had sold signs on them and others displayed price tags. Lorraine was shocked at the amount on the price tags. She realized she could have never afforded the picture he gave her.

Wow, I had no idea Guy is a high-priced artist. He is such an unassuming kind of guy. If he gets even ten per cent of each picture sold, and I'm sure it's a lot more, then the man must be wealthy. What could he possibly want to hang around with someone like me for? It's apparently not sex. Surely he can afford to have his motorhome fixed in a shop, so he doesn't need a traveling mechanic. Eventually, I have to tell him about my background and then he'll drop me like a hot potato. That's probably what he wants, someone to play with then humiliate. Well, I'll just keep my guard up and the thick wall around me. I will not let him hurt me. No, I will not let him hurt me.

The gallery was getting hot with all the body heat and the hot air coming out of everyone's mouth. Everyone was trying to impress everyone else with their knowledge of art.

People bragged to each other about how much they had spent on paintings and sculpture. With all the loud talk and puffery circulating around in the room, and all the women crowding around Guy, trying to get his attention, she could see that when he said he was ready for the attack, he really meant it.

Unnoticed, she stepped out of the gallery and walked down the street, enjoying the cool night air. Suddenly, she was grabbed from behind and, with her mouth covered, dragged into an alley.

"If you scream, I'll kill you," said a deep voice.

She could feel a cold steel blade on her neck. The hand was removed from her mouth and the man turned her to face him.

He wore a dark ski mask over his face.

"What do you want?" she whispered. "I only have a few dollars I can give you."

"I want you. I want sex," he said, while grabbing and raising her skirt.

"If that is all you want, you can have it. I haven't had a man since I was diagnosed with AIDS. Here, let me help you do it."

"You have AIDS?"

"Yes."

The man took off running. "Where are you going, honey?" she called after him.

Lorraine straightened her dress and hurried back to the gallery. She made her way through the crowd and approached Guy.

"Guy, can I have to key to the motorhome. I'm tired and want to go."

"Here, just leave the door unlocked. I'll be along in about a half an hour."

Lorraine went in the motorhome and locked the door behind her. She sat in the dark in shock. One second her mind was full of past life events, the next it was totally blank. She sat staring wide-eyed at the galley across the street. Then she closed her eyes and the masked dark face and the threatening words of "I'll kill you" resounded in her brain.

I should call the police. He'll go and grab another woman. Maybe right at this moment. What about Guy? How will it look for him if he comes out of the gallery with a crowd of admirers and here is his motorhome surrounded by police? What shall I do? Oh, Lord, what shall I do?

Lorraine sat there for about an hour. She didn't know if was hours or minutes. She lost track of all time. She heard someone trying to open the door. Her first reaction was frightened shock, then she remembered Guy did not have a key. "Who is it?"

"Me, Guy, please open the door." She unlocked the door and turned on a light. Guy came in looking surprised. "I thought you would be in bed by now."

"No. Guy, I have something to tell you."

"Oh?" He could tell from her voice that it was not good.

"Someone attempted to rape me."

"In the gallery?"

"No, I got hot and went outside. Walking down the street, I was grabbed from behind and dragged into an alley. He held a knife to my throat and said that if I screamed, he'd kill me."

"Oh my God, were you hurt? How did you get away?"

"I wasn't hurt. I told him that I would let him do it. That I haven't had a man since I was diagnosed with AIDS. Of course, I don't have AIDS, but me telling him that scared him away in a hurry."

"Smart girl, but you should have called the police."

"I thought about it, but I did not want your mo-torhome surrounded by cop cars when everyone came out of the gallery. I just sat here in the dark, thinking."

"You should have told me when I gave you the keys."

"I didn't want to spoil your evening. You looked like you were having so much fun."

"I call it work. It goes with the turf of being a famous artist. Those receptions stopped being fun a long time ago."

"Until tonight, I didn't know you are a famous art-ist."

"That's what I like about you. It is hard to come across someone who is not married to the Internet. It is really refreshing to meet someone like you. Now let's call the police and report that crime."

Since the rapist was unsuccessful with Lorraine, only one police car was sent to the motorhome. The older male cop and young female cop both were sympathetic to her and her recent ordeal. They both laughed when she told then how she got the perpetrator to run away.

"Would you mind being interviewed by the newspaper? I think more girls should know how to chase off an attempted rapist." asked the female cop.

"I won't mind, as long as they don't mention my name. Or will you, Guy?" she asked, looking at him.

"No, I don't want my name mentioned either, otherwise someone will just say it's a publicity stunt. I don't need any more publicity, especially the negative kind. Just tell the reporter to get here early, or they will only find a vacant parking space."

When the police left, Guy took Lorraine into his arms and told her he was so sorry.

"You have nothing to be sorry about. I was safe in the gallery. It's just that it was hot and stuffy and I needed some fresh air. I should have been aware of my surroundings. I only have myself to blame."

"It's not your fault. It just is a shame that a woman can't walk any street she wants to at any time of day or night. You sure are brave. Most women would be in hysterics having experienced what you just did." He held her, stroked her hair, and kissed her gently on her face. "Lorraine, my love, you are so brave."

Suddenly, she felt exhausted. "I've had a long day. I really need to get some sleep."

Silently he walked her to the door of the aft stateroom, said good night, and closed the door behind her.

The next morning while they were eating breakfast in the rig, a young reporter knocked on the door. She joined them for coffee and a bun while she asked questions and took notes. By the time her bun was consumed, she was done with the questions.

"It certainly was a pleasure to meet both of you," she said, extending her hand. "I wish you a very pleasant journey. Where are you going next?"

"That is undetermined," Guy said, not wishing to get into a lengthy conversation about what he should visit. "We are ready to shove off now. Thank you for coming, and if you don't mind, please mail me a copy of the article," he said, handing her a business card with his PO box address.

"Thank you, I'll do that."

"Now remember, do not mention either of our names in the article."

"My word of honor, I won't."

He escorted her out of the coach.

"The owner of the galley will bring me my check this morning. That should be before he opens the gallery at nine. First, I'll go to the bank and deposit my check, then we'll hit the road."

"Did you do well yesterday?"

"Better than I deserve."

"Great! Where are we going next?" she asked.

"Have you ever been to the Wisconsin Dells?"

"No,"

"Then today we go there."

℘℘℘

By ten in the morning, all the business was concluded and they were on the road toward the Wisconsin Dells. Lorraine was surprised that the place was so crowded with tourists. They were able to find a campground in a park. They enjoyed parking surrounded by forest and quiet. Normally, Lorraine would be eager to walk in the forest alone, but after the experience yesterday, she did not want to walk by herself anywhere.

I hope I will overcome this and stop being afraid. Last week I was shot at, and yesterday someone attempted to rape me. Things come in three. I wonder what is next. Stop it, stop thinking negative. If you're waiting for something bad to happen, it will. Only good will come my way from now on. All you bad stuff, I turn my back to you. Get away from me, I don't want you.

While Guy was sitting outside doing an oil painting, she called her mother.

"It's about time you called," Mary said. "We got a post card from Jimmy."

"Great news, where is he?"

"The card says Napoli, where is that?"

"That means Naples, Italy. What does he say?"

"He is enjoying the cruise. He says the guys on the ship tease him a lot, but there is one sailor with a sister in the Air Force Academy and he treats him with respect. He likes the city and has gone to some great museums. That's all he says."

"That's good news. Have you heard from my girls?"

"No, neither one. But on the other hand, I didn't tell them my address either nor give them my new phone number. I was afraid to after the shooting incident in Yuma."

"I think that's smart. If they want to reach you, they can write to your old address and have the post office forward it."

"If I know teenagers, they won't even bother. Now tell me, how are things going with you and Guy?"

"Yesterday, he had a gallery showing. Mom, I did not know it, but the man is a famous artist."

"I suppose you haven't told him about yourself yet."

"No, I will eventually."

"Meanwhile enjoy the ride."

"Mom, that doesn't sound nice. What do you mean by that?"

"When he learns your background, you can expect *sayonara*."

"Then I'll come back to Phoenix, get a job, and go on with my life. Meanwhile, I do enjoy the ride, as you put it. How are you enjoying your new apartment?"

"It's nice. There are nice people living in this senior housing complex and I'm making new friends. There is a real pretty Catholic church near here and a very friendly congregation. I should have moved here a long time ago."

"You have not been eligible that long. I suppose you are one of the younger residents there."

"One thing about being among old people, it makes me feel young. I got to go now. They're showing a new movie down in the rec hall. Good bye."

"Good bye, Mom."

When Lorraine concluded the call she felt a bit hungry. She looked in the fridge and saw the rest of the ingredients for tuna fish salad. She stepped outside and went to where Guy was painting. "Guy, would you like me to make some tuna fish salad? We could eat that for lunch on those wonderful rolls we got this morning?"

"Sounds good to me. What do you think? You like the painting?"

"Beautiful, and you're so fast."

"One thing is missing. I need to put a beautiful woman right over there." He pointed to a spot on the picture. "Would you go over there and stand near that rock until I say so?"

She walked into the sunshine and stood there for a few minutes. "Okay," he called, "you can move now."

She looked at the picture and saw herself standing in the beautiful landscape, wearing shorts and a tee shirt.

"There, now you are my model."

She chuckled. "I'm glad you don't do nudes."

Chapter 21

The next day they were crossing the Mississippi River into Iowa, when Lorraine's cell phone rang. "It's my mother," she announced before answering. "Hi, Mom, What's up?"

"Lori, something terrible happened," Mary said between sobs. "Your daughter Rachel was in a terrible car wreck and she is in a hospital. I got a call from a nurse there."

"Mom, please calm down and tell me what is going on. What do you know? Where is she at?"

"She's in Austin. She stayed in school for the summer to get ahead of her classes, at least that what she had told me a few weeks ago. I really think she needed to make up some classes, but that's beside the point now. I figured I had to tell you. I know she did not want to see you, but now that she's in critical condition, I thought you would want to know."

"Of course, I'd want to know. After all, she is my child. What hospital is she at?"

"Let's see now, I wrote it down." Lorraine could hear her fumbling through some papers. "Yes, here it is. She's in the Seton Medical Center. Do you think that is a Catholic hospital?"

"I don't know. I'm in Iowa. What do you expect me to do?"

"All I know is, if it was you in her condition, I would go and see you. What you do is up to you," she said coldly.

"Thanks, Mom, for telling me. If you learn any news, please let me know. I'll let you know what I'll do next when I decide." The line buzzed. "We are fading. Bye, Mom, and thanks for calling." She turned to Guy. "My daughter, who wanted nothing to do with me, is lying in a hospital in critical condition, at least that's what my mother says about her condition. I have to decide what I want to do."

"There is a rest stop ahead. I'll pull her over. We need to talk about this." He drove into a rest area and parked next to another motorhome. "It was time to take a break anyway," he said, getting up and walking back to the refrigerator.

He pulled out a can of V8 and started drinking.

"Now I suppose you want to go see your daughter."

"I do but she is so far away. I don't want you to miss your next showing."

"We'll talk about that later. The question is, do you want to go to your daughter?"

"I really do. I haven't seen her for sixteen years." Then she put her hand in front of her mouth, feeling embarrassed.

Guy looked at her very intensely. "Why do you look so ashamed?"

Lorraine looked down at her hands on the table. "I never did tell you much about myself. I suppose I should have right off the bat. I hope you'll forgive me. I didn't lie to you, but neither did I tell you that I am an ex-con. I was in jail for manslaughter. There, I said it. Now you're going to put me out and drive away." Tears came to her eyes.

"Lorraine, my dear, I'm not going to put you out here. The least I would do is drop you off at a bus stop." He chuckled. "I know, this is no time to joke with you, but I couldn't help it. No, my dear." He took both of her hands in his. "I know all about your back ground."

"You do? How is that?"

"Internet. I can get all that vital information on my new phone. I know when and where you were born, who your parents are, whom you married, the speeding ticket you got, about your husband abusing you, and how he died. And that you were sent to prison for fifteen years.

There you learned to be an auto mechanic and are certified. Anything else you want to know about yourself?"

"Yes, I really want to know why you are hanging around with me."

"I see qualities in you that you are overlooking yourself. I see a loving, caring person—a women who is not only beautiful in an unassuming way, but smart. I like that you have talents and are thrifty. I am looking for a wife, not a one night stand. I know I'm getting up there, but I told myself long ago that I wanted to be married by the time I'm forty. That gives me one more year. I know I could get some young chick, but I'm not interested in that. I want a mature woman, and one, hopefully, who is still willing to have at least one more baby." He paused and studied her. "I hope the woman I'm looking at this very moment feels that she could make a life with me."

Lorraine was shocked and words would not come out of her mouth, no matter how hard she tried.

"One more thing I want to add." he said. "When I first saw you and you came into my motorhome for that fish dinner, I wanted to take you into my bed right then and there. But I stopped myself from trying to even start. I saw you as a potential wife, not a one night stand. I'm not much of a church-going man, but to me a woman's body is sacred."

"I have never heard a man speak that way."

"Well then, listen and hear what I say. Life starts in a woman and that is a holy thing. Sure, sex can be pleasurable. I'm sure God designed it that way for a purpose, but it should not be treated as a toy. If two people have sex too soon, they lose their objectivity and try to make the other person fit, even if they are wrong for each other. True love is not infatuation. Infatuation comes and goes quickly. True love lasts even through hard times. Also, if one gives in too easily, it sends a message. So many women nowadays do not understand that. I have even heard them brag about how many men they have slept with. To me, that's not something they should be proud of."

"I can honestly say the only man I have ever been intimate with was my husband."

"I knew I picked well. At the moment, I am not ready to propose marriage to you, but I hope we can build on our relationship and, if it continues the way it has been going, I hope you will have me and then consent to being my wife."

"Wow, Guy. I believe I have deep feelings for you, too. You are a very wise and special man. I am honored that you feel this way about me. Now the question is, how will I get to Austin? I think I have enough money with me to take a bus there."

"My dear, you are sitting in the bus. If we take turns driving, we should be there within twenty four hours."

"But what about your showing in Des Moines?"

"I'll call and say I have a family emergency and do it another time. If they insist on the showing, I'll just ship them some more pictures and they can go on without me."

"I think you just have to find a double for yourself."

"Hey, that is a good idea. I might just do that." He laughed, took her in his arms, and slowly kissed her.

Lorraine was both shocked and flattered. She really did not expect the man to look at her as a potential wife. She was not even that enthused about getting married in the near future and then having another child or two. She knew her biological clock was rapidly approaching midnight. She decided to make up her mind quickly if he was the man for her and if she really wanted another husband, at least right now.

"If we want to get to Austin," he said, "we better hit the road and really burn some rubber. Are you ready to go?"

"As ready as I'll ever be. Do you really trust me to drive your rig?"

"You drove the other one okay. I'm sure you can handle this one. Get behind the wheel right now, adjust the seat if necessary, and drive."

⌀⌀⌀

Lorraine was surprised at how nicely the motorhome drove. At times, she was also able to sit in the passenger seat and catch some cat naps.

They changed drivers about every two hours and

were able to make it to Seaton Medical Center in one day.

At the front desk she was asked what her relationship was to the patient.

"I'm her mother."

"It says here, that her mother is in the room with her. How can she have two mothers?"

"Most likely, someone forgot to write grandmother." Lorraine pulled out her driver's license to confirm her name. She was given directions to the room.

In the elevator taking her to the fifth floor Lorraine started shaking.

"Hold together now. In a few minutes, you'll see your daughter," Guy said gently.

"It's not the daughter I'm afraid of, it's the mother-in-law. I bet she is sitting by the bed acting as the suffering mother. What will she do to me?"

"I'm here to protect you."

"And I'm so glad."

Rachel was lying in a small room with a single bed. The curtain of the large glass window from the hall was open and the first thing Lorraine saw was a young woman hooked up to tubes going in and out of her body. Sitting on a chair next to the bed was another person.

Only the top of the head with black hair was visible from behind. Lorraine's heart accelerated its beat.

"Elena?"

The woman turned in the chair and glared at Lorraine. "It's you. What do you want here?"

"To see my daughter. How is she doing? What do the doctors say?"

"She might not make it." Then Elena started to cry.

Lorraine took her daughter's hand and felt no response. *At least she is not pulling her hand away.* She looked at Guy standing in the doorway looking very sympathetic.

"Elena, I hope you can forgive me for what has gone on in the past."

"You fiend, you killed my only child. I can never forgive you."

"Elena, I will only say this once. I feared he would have killed me. It was strictly self-defense. Please see it in your heart to forgive. The past cannot be changed, but the future can. I know you love Rachel and so do I. Please let us work together to do what is best for her."

Elena looked at Lorraine without expression. "You and I will never be friends, but for the sake of Rachel and the other two, I'll try to get along."

"Thank you, Elena, and I want you to meet my friend, Guy Walcott," Lorraine said, pointing to him. "Guy, meet my mother-in-law, Elena."

"Pleased to meet you, ma'am."

"Gracias, now you better get out of the doorway, the doctor is here."

In walked a woman of about fifty, wearing scrubs and a stethoscope around her neck.

"You must be her sister," she said to Lorraine. "I'm Dr. Parr."

"No, I'm the mother, and this is the grandmother," Lorraine said. "And this is my friend Guy Walcott."

"Not *the* Guy Walcott, or are you?"

"I might be the one you think I am."

Elena looked puzzled. Then the doctor continued. "I'm familiar with your work. Even have one of your water colors in my office."

"Tell you what, Doctor, you get our girl through this and your watercolor will get a companion."

The doctor saw the puzzled expression on Elena's face. "This man here is a very famous artist."

Elena flashed a quick smile. "What is the status with my daughter—I mean, granddaughter?"

"She has extensive internal injuries, which we could repair pretty well. The worst is neither of her kidneys could be saved. We can put her on a UNOS list and, if we are lucky, find a match in a few months or even years. Meanwhile, she needs to be on dialysis. She's still in a coma, but I expect her to wake up soon."

"What does UNOS stand for?" Elena asked.

"United Network for Organ Sharing," answered the doctor.

"I'll be willing to give her one of my kidneys," Elena said quickly. "I love that girl and will do anything for her."

"We will need to do a blood test and cross match.

You can get that done in the lab right now."

"I volunteer to donate one of my kidneys, too," Lorraine said quickly, moving toward the door.

Both women took off toward the lab.

"While you ladies are in the lab, I'll find the cafeteria and get some lunch," Guy said. "Do you want to meet me there when you get done?"

"I'll do that. I'm hungry, too," Lorraine said.

While the women sat in the lab across from each other, both getting their blood drawn, Lorraine smiled at Elena. There was acknowledgment with a slight nod. That little gesture gave her such happiness.

It is a new beginning.

After lunch, all three met in Rachel's room. When they entered, Rachel's eyes were flickering. Elena rushed to her side and took her hand.

"Rachel, my dear, Mommy is here. Wake up, darling."

As soon as Lorraine realized that the word mommy did not apply to her, a sadness overcame her. The good feeling begun in the lab flew out of the window like a feather on a breeze.

I should expect that. I have not been in the girl's life for almost sixteen years. She considers Elena her mother. Lorraine just watched as her daughter slowly opened her eyes and looked at Elena. A faint smile crossed her face before she closed her eyes again. After a while, Dr. Parr entered.

"Ladies, Mr. Walcott, I have good news. One of you is a match."

I hope it's Elena. I really don't want to part with any of my body. Why did I volunteer? Was it to get back into Elena's graces? What if I am the match? Will I go through with it? My daughter hates me. Am I willing to donate a kidney? My fate is in the hands of God. If I am the one, so be it.

Dr. Parr looked at both women who looked anxiously into her face. "Mrs. Lopez, you are the match," she said, looking at Lorraine.

"Which Mrs. Lopez are you talking about? We both have that name," Elena asked.

"The younger one, or should I just say the biological mother."

"So, I'm a match. What happens next?" Lorraine asked anxiously.

"We need to give Rachel a few days to recover from her surgery two days ago," the doctor told them. "Also, you will need to be evaluated by a psychiatrist. We have an excellent transplant surgeon affiliated with this hospital. As a matter of fact, he is checking on a patient in the next room. This would be a good time for you to meet him." Dr. Parr rushed out the door. A few minutes later she returned with a young doctor in tow. "This is Dr. Thompson," she said, motioning with her hand. "And this is Lorraine Lopez who is a match and willing to donate a kidney."

The young doctor's face was a contrast of features. He looked much younger than his years. As if trying to hide the fact, he made up for the thin hair on his head with bushy mutton-chop sideburns almost meeting his blond mustache. The back of his light brown hair hung over his collar. His sky blue eyes radiated a deep intelligence. He spoke in a calm confident voice as he shook Lorraine's hand and gave a general nod to the other two people in the room.

"You are a hero, Mrs. Lopez. It will mean a life for your daughter rather than being hooked to a dialysis machine three times a week. There are several steps to go through but, if all goes well, we should be able to perform the surgery in about a week."

Rachel opened her eyes. The young doctor saw it, moved next to her, and took her hand. "Young lady, I'm Dr. Thompson. You are one lucky young woman. We have found a donor for a kidney."

"Who?" she asked in a soft voice.

"Your mother," the doctor answered.

Rachel looked at Elena. "Not me, darling, but your real mother," Elena said, pointing toward Lorraine.

Rachel followed her gaze and gave her mother a confused look. "You? You would do that?"

"Of course, I would," Lorraine said, moving closer and taking her hand. "A mother will do anything for her child."

"After the way I treated you?" Then she closed her eyes.

Dr. Thompson's pager vibrated. He looked at it. "Nice meeting you all. I have to go now." And he hurried out of the room.

∽◌∽

That evening, in the motorhome parked on the hospital parking lot, Lorraine and Guy were alone drinking a glass of wine.

"Guy, I was really hoping I would not be a match. Do you think that is terrible of me?"

"Of course not. To have a perfectly healthy part of the body removed is not a cheerful thought by any stretch of the imagination. I only know one person in this world I would do that for."

"Who is that?"

"I'm looking at her."

"Oh, Guy, you would? How sweet of you." She blew him a kiss. "I'm going to undergo some rigorous examinations. I'll be tied up most of the next few days. I hope you won't get too bored sitting around here."

"I never get bored. I have my oils and watercolor to keep me occupied. Don't worry about me. After the hard pushing to get here, it's a relief not having to drive for a while."

Lorraine yawned. "I'm really tired, if you don't mind, I'm going to turn in early."

"Me too. All we've had are a few little cat naps in the last two days. Not to mention the stress and tension you have been going through. I have a feeling that good will come out of this."

"I think that has already started. Not only does my daughter know I'm alive, but Elena spoke to me in a civil manner. I don't hold it against her for being angry with me. After all, Alex was her only child and she had no idea what a monster he could be. I'm going to say good night and go off to bed."

"Good night, sweetheart." He rose to give her a kiss. "You are the bravest woman I know."

Lorraine lay in bed, staring at the ceiling. *Oh, Guy, I wish you were here besides me. I might die during the surgery. Before I die I would like to have sex at least once more. Can he possibly deny me that?* She rubbed her lower stomach. It again had that increasingly achy feeling. *Oh, Guy, I need you. I want you.*

Chapter 22

Two days later, Lorraine had a consultation with the young transplant surgeon. In his calm professional voice, that could have been the voice of an angel, he told her that her pap smear concerned him.

"Do you have pain during intercourse?"

Lorraine was shocked by the question. She did not quite know how to answer him. She looked around the room.

"Well do you? Don't be embarrassed to tell me."

"I have not had any intercourse for over fifteen years."

A split second of surprise fluttered across his face, although he tried to keep a serious demeanor.

"Over fifteen years? Do you have a living will or

someone with medical power of attorney? Is there some-one who can speak for you medically?"

"Not at the moment, but I'll ask my friend if he wants to be that. In case push comes to shove, you will be able to speak with him."

Guy and Lorraine sat in the business office signing a ton of papers. Since she had no job, she had no insurance. Lorraine signed a document that she would be responsible for any unpaid procedures that were not connected with the transplant. *I'll pay any bill. It might take me a hundred years, but I do pay my debts.*

After the business was concluded, she again went to visit with her daughter. Rachel was alone, sitting up in bed eating a light meal. She smiled when her mother entered.

"Mom, thanks for coming. Hello, Guy, good to see you. Are you ready for tomorrow?"

"As ready as I'll ever be."

"Mom, I do want to apologize for not having come to see you when you came to San Marcos. I hope you forgive me."

"Of course I forgive you. I can understand why you felt that way."

"Yes, I heard nothing but bad about you. Well, I can't say that, Grandma Albright tried to talk nice about you. But she had to watch every word she said because she was afraid her visiting rights would be taken away."

"That is all behind us. The heaviest thing to carry is a

grudge. Shake it off. The past cannot be changed but you can make it a better future."

"Oh, Mom, you are so wise."

"I had a lot of time to do a lot of thinking. I always said, no matter what the situation or how bad it looks, we have to turn it around and extract the good out of it. Now sleep well, my child, tomorrow is a big day for both of us."

e∽ce∽

The next day, she walked with Guy the short distance from the motorhome toward the main entrance of the hospital. "Guy, when I crouched behind the garbage can getting shot at, I was not as afraid as I am this very moment. I have never had surgery before."

"You'll be fine. Just think, you now have a daughter again, and in Yuma is your other daughter, eager for your return. You again have a relationship with your mother-in-law. Everything will turn out just fine. I'll pray for you."

"That is the first time you've told me that you pray. You are religious."

"I don't call myself religious but spiritual. I certainly believe in God. Look around, look at the blue sky, take a deep breath of God's clean air. God is with you. I will be there when you wake up, if they let me."

"I hope so," she said, giving him one last kiss. Then they parted.

Guy and Elena were both sitting in the lounge outside surgery. It was not long before the surgeon, Dr. Moreno, came out to speak with Guy.

"The kidney was removed and is now in the process of being transplanted," said the handsome surgeon. "However, we have a problem with Lorraine."

"What is that?" Guy asked anxiously, walking with the doctor toward a private corner of the room.

"She has a very large fibroid tumor on her uterus. It's the kind of tumor that would soon go into cancer. It is my strong recommendation that we do a hysterectomy. Of course, you know that means no more children—in case you had such plans."

"If she was your wife, what would you do?"

"I would not hesitate for a moment and have the hysterectomy. Even if we remove the tumor alone, pregnancy would not be very likely and the danger of cancer is very real."

"Then do it. Do the hysterectomy."

"You are sure?"

"I am sure."

"It will be done. She should come out of surgery in about an hour. You can see her briefly in the recovery room."

"Thank you, doctor."

Guy went and told Elena the status. Elena nodded and resumed her rosary.

He was sitting next to the bed in the recovery room when Lorraine slowly came to.

"Hello, sweetheart, how are you feeling?"

"I hurt like hell."

"Nurse, please, my fiancée is in pain," Guy said to the nearest nurse.

The nurse took a syringe and injected pain killer into an IV tube going into the patient's arm.

Lorraine smiled. She heard him refer to her as his fiancée. That sounded nice.

In her private room, Lorraine went in and out of conscientiousness. Sometimes she felt someone fussing over her and peeked at the nurse. Then she was alone again. Eventually a doctor came to see her. She had her eyes closed when she was tapped on the hand.

"Lorraine, wake up, I need to talk with you. This is Dr. Moreno."

She opened her eyes and looked at the handsome young man with dark curls spilling over his forehead. She smiled. "You are too young and handsome to be a doctor."

The doctor chuckled. "If you want to see my diploma from Johns Hopkins Medical School, I'll rush to my office and get it for you."

"I'll just take your word for it."

"Lorraine, I need to tell you that it was necessary to

perform a hysterectomy on you. The tumor in your uterus was large and to the stage where it would go malignant. We took out the uterus and fallopian tubes. The ovaries looked good so they were left in."

"Oh no," Lorraine cried. "Guy was planning on getting married and we were going to have another baby. Now I'm damaged goods. I'll probably never see him again."

"No, that's not true. You are not damaged goods. No one will be able to look at you and say, see, this woman has no uterus."

"And only one kidney," Lorraine added.

"I consulted with Guy before the procedure and he said to go ahead and do the surgery. Remember, you gave him that power."

"My life is over now," Lorraine said, crying softly.

"No it's not." Dr. Moreno handed her a Kleenex, "You are young and beautiful even without a uterus. Now there is someone here to see you."

"Guy?" she asked hopefully.

"No, it's a young lady," the doctor said.

In walked Rachel with a big smile.

"Rachel, you're up. How do you feel?"

"Better, a lot better. When I got the new kidney, I immediately felt better. The doctor says it is functioning well. Mom, I'll be forever grateful." Rachel bent over and kissed Lorraine on the cheek. "Thank you, Mom, thank you for everything."

"Having found the tumor when we did could possibly have saved your life," Dr. Moreno continued. The doctor's pager went off. He looked at it. "I have to go. I'm needed in Emergency. I'll see you later." And he rushed out of the room.

Rachel took her mother's hand. "Don't cry, Mom, everything will be okay."

"It would be if Guy were here. I thought I would never love again, but that's not the way it went. I thought Guy loved me, but now that I'm damaged goods, he took off."

There was a knock on the door. "May I come in?"

Lorraine looked up and saw Elena entering with a big bouquet of flowers. "Lorraine, how are you feeling?"

"Still pretty sore. I'm glad you came, Elena."

"I take back a statement I made over a week ago,"

"What was that?"

"That we'd never be friends. Please accept my apology and maybe we can share our family like we should."

"Apology accepted. What about Juan? Will he get along with me?"

"Lorraine, when I tell him to, he will love you, too. You have saved our Rachel's life."

"Yes, Mom, being hooked up to dialysis is certainly no fun. I will have to be extremely careful for the next several months and not be exposed to bad germs, but I can feel alive."

"Elena," Lorraine said, looking at her pleadingly, "could you do me a big favor?"

"Just name it."

"Go to the parking lot and see if Guy's motorhome is there and what he might be doing?"

"Sure, I'll do that. I know where it is." She left the room.

"Mom, I've been up enough now, I'll just go back to bed and take a nap. I'll see you later."

"Yes dear, you do that. I don't want you overdoing it."

A short time later Elena returned. Lorraine could tell from her expression that the news was not good.

"Lorraine, the motorhome is gone. I'm so sorry that didn't work out for you." She handed her a Kleenex as Lorraine started to cry.

"That bastard, that damn bastard, took off without even having the decency to say goodbye. That goes to show you, a man can't be trusted." Lorraine's wails became louder. "He said he loved me, the lying bastard. He said he was thinking of us marrying and possibly having a baby. Now that I'm damaged goods, it's *sayonara.*"

"I have my cell phone. Tell me his number, and I'll try to call."

Lorraine did remember his number and Elena dialed.

"All I'm getting is voice mail saying his box is full. I'm sorry."

"Here I am, stranded in Austin. I'm out of money, lying in a hospital, feeling rotten and abandoned. I wish I would just have died."

"Don't say that. I'm here and your daughter is here. Don't you have a cell phone to call out?"

"That's right. It should be in the closet there with my clothes. Please, Elena, see if you can find it." Elena found it but the battery was dead. "And my charger is in the motorhome along with my clothes and all. I can't believe that man just taking off and leaving me here stranded with nothing."

"If you want to call your mother, you can use my phone. And as far as getting back to Yuma, you can go with me and Rachel. We plan to rent a car and drive. We can talk about that later."

"Elena, would you be so kind and call my mother and give her an update on my and Rachel's condition? Just don't say anything about Guy."

"I'll do that. Then I'll leave you in privacy for a while. I'll be in the cafeteria getting a bite to eat. I'll see you later." Elena bent over and kissed her on the forehead.

Lorraine wept as Elena left the room.

Chapter 23

Lorraine was still crying when a nurse entered. "How are we doing?" she asked cheerfully, "Are you in pain dear? I can help you with that."

"Not with the pain I have. If you could give a shot for that, I'd take a hundred."

"I'm afraid we don't have any remedy for that. Sorry. Lunch will be served soon. We have you on light food now."

"I'm not hungry."

"Please try, you must eat something. You don't want to starve to death."

"That's just what I want. Why prolong the agony? Just let me starve to death."

The nurse took Lorraine's hand. "There, there, having a hysterectomy is not the end of the world. In a few days, you'll feel like a new person."

An aide entered the room and put a tray of food in front of Lorraine. After a while she picked up a spoon and started eating the orange Jell-O. Soon that was consumed and she picked at the rest of the food on the tray. When she looked up she saw a big bouquet of red roses in the door frame.

Just the roses, no one else.

"Who is there?" she called.

"Guess," answered a deep voice.

"Justin Bieber?"

"Close." And the figure of a man stepped into the doorway, holding the flowers in front of his face.

"Guy, is it really you?" Lorraine called with a lurch of excitement. "Oh, Guy, I thought you took off on me."

"Take off on you? No way." He rushed toward the bed and took her in his arms, kissing her gently on the lips. "I had to take the RV to a facility. There were two full tanks and one empty one, you know what I mean. As it turns out, the place was pretty far away and I got caught by tons of traffic going through a construction site. I called the front desk of the hospital, leaving a message for you after trying your number with no success."

"I didn't get any message."

"I really wanted to be here when you woke up this morning, but figured it would only take me about an hour to do what I needed to do and I would be back in time.

Well I was wrong. I'm sorry. I hope you didn't worry too much."

"Now that you are here, everything is all right," she said, giving him an adoring look, "and I'm hungry." She returned her attention to the tray of food.

"I haven't eaten at all yet today. I'll be in the cafeteria for a while. They do have good food here. I'll be back in a little while."

"I'm not going anywhere," she said with a laugh.

ౚౚౚ

The next day Guy, Elena, and Rachel were all visiting with Lorraine in her private room. The discussion was how everyone would return to Arizona.

"I'll be glad to take you back in the motorhome," Guy offered. "But I will have to stop in Albuquerque at my house for a while."

"I believe," Elena said, "that Rachel and I will be better off just renting a big comfortable car and driving back. We should be able to get home in three days. Thank you for the offer anyway." She gave Lorraine a wink.

Lorraine blushed.

"Lorraine, there is something I would like to ask you," Guy said. "I would like both of you ladies to hear the question too."

"Oh, what is that?" Lorraine asked.

Guy moved the straight chair he was sitting on as

close to the bed as possible and took Lorraine's left hand in both of his. He looked into her hazel eyes and said in a low voice, "Lorraine, I love you. Will you marry me?"

Lorraine looked intensely into his eyes then whispered, "Yes, Guy, I will marry you."

"You make me the happiest man alive." Then he reached into his pants pocket and pulled out a silver band made of twisted wire. He put the ring on her finger. "It fits. I made that ring many years ago planning to give it to the woman I would marry. I said to myself then, if this ring fits, there will be no doubt that she is the right one."

"Oh Guy, it's beautiful, thank you."

Elena looked at it critically. "That looks like a poor people's ring."

"I think it's beautiful, especially since he made it himself." Lorraine looked at Guy, "I will always treasure it."

"That was rude of me," Elena said. "Forgive me, and you two seal the event with a kiss."

"It's okay, Elena," Guy said. "Good idea." And he gently planted a kiss on Lorraine's lips. Next he gave Rachel a hug and then Elena.

"We welcome you to the family," Rachel said. "When are you planning on getting married?"

"That is up to your mother, but it can't be too soon for me."

"If you need a bridesmaid, I'm volunteering," Rachel said. "But now I better get my rest and leave you two lovebirds alone. Come, *Abuela,* walk me back to my room."

"Yes, Rachel dear," Elena said as they left the room.

"Alone at last," Lorraine said with a happy smile. "This has been some week. First, I reconnected with my daughter and learned my other daughter is eager to see me. My mother-in-law is now my friend, and, best of all, you want to marry me. I could not be happier. Guy, please hug and pinch me, so I know this is real."

"It is real," he assured her while hugging her gently. "Now you better get your rest. You want to leave this hospital as soon as possible and go on with our life."

"Yes, I am ready for a nap. I'll see you later," she said, closing her eyes with a happy smile on her face.

℘ℑ℘ℑ

A few days later Guy was in the hospital room along with Dr. Moreno as he signed the release papers.

"You will be able to travel, but please—" He looked at Guy. "Keep the amount of daily mileage down. Let her rest preferably without the bumps and jiggles of the road. And when you get to where you're going, make an appointment with a doctor for a final check-up. Where is it you are going?"

"My home's in Albuquerque," Guy said, "and I have a good physician I'll take her to."

A nurse pushing a wheel chair entered. "It was nice

meeting you. Good luck and have a happy marriage."

The doctor handed Lorraine some papers, a box of pills, and a prescription for pain pills. "Take these only if you feel you need them. Good bye then."

"Thank you for all you have done for me," said Lorraine, reaching out to hug the doctor.

Then she took a seat in the wheel chair with the large bouquet of red roses on her lap. The nurse wheeled her away with Guy walking behind.

The young nurse stayed with her in the lobby while Guy went to get the motorhome.

"You sure have a handsome and nice man. I too wish you many happy years together."

"Thank you, I hope it works out."

"You sound apprehensive."

"Getting married is a big step, and I won't be able to give him what he really wants."

"What is that?" asked the nurse.

"Guy was hoping for children, at least one. I'm afraid he just feels sorry for me. Who knows if there ever will be a wedding?" Tears came to Lorraine's eyes.

"The way he looks at you, I would say the man really loves you. Don't you worry. Everything will turn out all right, I just know it."

"I wish I could feel more confident," Lorraine said as the thirty-two foot motorhome drove up.

The nurse wheeled her to the curb and helped Lorraine up the steps into the motorhome. She looked around in the rig. "Nice coach. Maybe I can talk my husband into buying one. I would love to travel that way."

"Yes, it is a comfortable way to travel," said Guy, who was securing the vase of flowers in the galley sink. "And one meets the nicest people in the campgrounds."

Lorraine sat down in the passenger seat. The nurse left. Guy pushed in the steps and locked the side door. Then he got into the driver's seat. "Alone at last with my sweetheart." He reached for her hand and kissed it. "There is a really nice campground not too far away. We'll go there before we go on. Okay with you?"

"Sounds good."

Guy drove cautiously through the heavy traffic onto a less traveled road going through the Texas Hill Country. They traveled, saying little. Lorraine absorbed the beauty of the landscapes and slowly realized that she was glad to be alive. *I hope the nurse is right, and everything will turn out all right.*

After hooking up the rig in a campground with grass and trees, Guy made lunch for them. He served chicken with sweet potatoes and green lettuce salad. Lorraine ate with gusto, relishing every morsel.

"I'm happy to see you enjoying food again."

"It's delicious, must be cooked with love."

"That it is," he said taking her hand and kissing it warmly.

Chapter 24

Slowly they made their way west toward Albuquerque. They usually ate lunch in a restaurant. After lunch, Lorraine would take a nap while Guy was making calls on his cell phone.

One afternoon he summarized his plans for the coming few weeks. "When we get to Albuquerque, we'll stay in my house for a while. My agent arranged for two showings in galleries there and another one in Santa Fe. I have also made a doctor appointment for you. I hope you are agreeable with that schedule."

"I don't know if I can face another gallery after what happened in Green Bay," Lorraine said with apprehension in her voice, thinking about the attempted rape.

"You can go if you wish or you can stay in my

house. I have a housekeeper who comes in twice a week and I can ask her to stay with you during the evening I'm at the art gallery"

"I really don't feel I need a baby sitter. I won't mind staying by myself."

"We don't have to decide that right now. I bet in another week you are going to be fully recovered."

"I feel ninety-five percent up to par right now."

"In that case, you can start planning a wedding," he said with excitement in his voice.

"I am hoping for a simple and small wedding," she answered. "What are your thoughts for that?"

"Just tell me where and when I need to be there."

"That's all. Don't you have family or friends to invite?"

"If I know them, they'll find out about it and show up. Planning a wedding is a woman's thing. I know you'll handle it."

"Number one, I want to have it in a Catholic church."

"That's fine. Just don't expect me to become a Catholic."

"You never did mention it. What is your faith?"

"I was raised Jewish, but fell away from that. I'm not one to follow the rituals. I believe in God, I live a decent life. I let God be my judge when it comes to an afterlife."

"Don't you believe in heaven and hell?"

"We make our own heaven and hell right here on

earth. Attitude plays a major role in our happiness. If we decide to love and be happy, we will be."

"Wow, I have never met anyone like you before. Have you ever read the Bible?"

"From cover to cover a number of times. The key lays in its interpretation. Five people can read the same passage and get five meanings out of it. If the Catholic Church satisfies your spiritual needs, fine, go there. I satisfy my spiritual needs by walking in God's creation and meditating while breathing his pure air. That is my church."

"I would like it if you go to church with me occasionally."

"I make you a deal, you go hiking with me on occasion, and I'll go to church with you now and then."

"That is agreeable with me," Lorraine said, taking both of his hands. "Let's seal the deal with a kiss."

"That is a delectable way to sign a contract," he said, wrapping his arms around her and kissing her again and again on the lips.

Lorraine felt his erection against her leg.

Hello, Junior, I was wondering if you would ever stir. Glad to know you are still alive.

∽∾∽

Lorraine had an idea that Guy was a well-paid artist. She imagined that he would live in a very large and opulent house in Albuquerque. *I wonder how his neighbors will treat me. I hope they are not snobs like the people I met at the showing in Green Bay. Will I be able to fit in, or will everyone just look down their noses at me? I will only decide then if I will be able to take being his wife. Meanwhile, I will not plan any wedding.*

If he decides I'm not good enough for him, all the planning would be wasted and the disappointment even greater. I hope I'm worrying for nothing, but I have to be prepared for the worst.

At the next fuel stop was a gift shop with magazines. She did pick up a bridal magazine. *I just want to see what the modern trends in weddings are,* she said to herself, and bought the magazine.

That evening they sat by candle light and music enjoying a glass of wine after dinner.

"If all goes well, tomorrow evening we should be home."

"You mean *you* should be home. At the moment, I still live in that RV park in Phoenix."

"I certainly hope that will change soon. I can't wait for us to be husband and wife."

"Are you really certain about that?" she asked with apprehension. "Please don't feel you have to marry me because you feel sorry for me. I know you wanted children and that is not on the menu now. I would love to give you a baby but—"

He cut the sentence short with a kiss.

"Actually, I have many children. You will meet them when we get home."

"Really?" she asked, shocked. "Who is their mother?"

"There are many mothers." He chuckled. "You'll see."

What is that man telling me? Does he have a harem?

He gave an amused chuckle when he saw the expression on her face. "It's quite all right. You'll like them."

Is this man playing with me? I will not get into any sticky situations. If I don't think I'm getting into a good situation, I'll just take a bus to Phoenix, move back into my motorhome, get a job as an auto mechanic, and enjoy a happy single life. Yes, I know I can be happy being single. I don't need a man.

Again Guy took her into his arms and kissed her passionately.

I can be happy being single, but being held and loved is so much better. She lay across his lap and felt his bulge on her back.

"In a few days," she said in a whisper, "we can try making love."

"I'll be ready when you are."

"I'm ready now, but doctor's orders are—"

"No sex until after your check-up. I'll be a good boy and wait."

I wonder how my life would be different if I would have waited when I was seventeen. Would Alex and I have gotten married? Probably, I was totally infatuated with him. Was it real love? Who knows what is real love and what is infatuation? That is the age-old question. Would Guy run into a burning building to rescue me? Would I run into a burning building to rescue him? Yeah, I think I would. I suppose that means real love. But what disturbs me is the fact that he says he has many children. Does that mean he fathered many children or does he mean something else? So many unanswered questions. Okay, Lorraine, enjoy the moment, the warmth of the candles, the soft music, and the wine giving you a little buzz. And it makes you feel good.

She put her arms around his neck and gave him a passionate kiss.

❧❧❧

It was late afternoon when the motorhome drove into the driveway of a private one-story Southwest-style home. The house was bigger than her mother's house, but not as large and opulent as the Lopez house in Yuma. Lorraine considered it a rather modest dwelling in a middle-class neighborhood.

"We are home," announced Guy with pleasure. He blew the horn and a middle aged Hispanic woman came out of the house with outstretched arms and a smile showing even white teeth.

"*Señor, me señor* so good to see you," she said giving him a hearty embrace. "Come in, come in, everything is ready for you."

"Nora, good to see you, too," Guy said, giving the woman a robust hug. "And this is Lorraine,"

"A pleasure meeting you, Miss Lorraine, Guy told me so much about you," she said, giving Lorraine a gentle hug.

"It's wonderful meeting you and to finally stop driving for a day or so," Lorraine said.

They followed the woman into the house. The interior was decorated in southwestern style with Guy's paintings and Indian rugs hanging on the walls. In the corner was an oval fireplace with a fire burning. Even though it was summer and warm out, the fire gave the house a welcoming atmosphere. From the open kitchen came the delicious aroma of cooking and baking.

"I hope you two are hungry. You can eat soon."

"I have been saving lots of room in my stomach for your cooking." Turning to Lorraine, he said, "Come with me and I show you to your room."

They went around a corner and Guy led her into the guest room. There were two single beds against the wall on opposite sides of the room.

A walk in closet was empty and so was an oak dresser with a mirror. The door to the bathroom stood open and Lorraine was struck by the gleaming, glaring colors of turquoise and orange.

"Thank you, this room will be fine."

"I'll bring your things in from the motorhome," Guy said, leaving.

Lorraine closed the bathroom door. The bedroom color was more to her liking, a pale turquoise accented with a little coral.

While Nora finished cooking, Guy showed Lorraine around his garden. It contained many trees, bushes, and plants. Some were in flower pots, most in the ground. Water flowed from a mount of rocks and fell into a pool, afterward trickling along the rocks into a small pond. Goldfish and koi swam in the pond. One had to follow the paths for the garden to be revealed a little at a time. At the back of the property was another building the size of a three car garage. They went inside.

"This is my studio," Guy said with a sweep of his arm. "You like it?"

Lorraine looked around and calculated that, from the prices she saw in the gallery, this room with skylights and high windows must contain over a million dollars' worth of art. Some pictures in an unfinished stage stood on easels.

"Wonderful. I suppose this is where you spend most of the day."

"There and downtown. I'll show you my other studio tomorrow. You'll like it."

As Guy was locking up the studio a humming bird buzzed at Lorraine's ear.

"He thinks the red flower earring you're wearing is a flower for him to get nectar."

"How cute. I like all those hummingbird feeders you have around. They are really doing their job. I've never seen so many hummingbirds in one place before."

"They are mostly attracted by the flowers," Guy said, watching several birds buzzing at a red lobelia.

"Your garden is the most peaceful place."

"God lives in my garden."

"I think you're right. I feel close to God too."

Hand in hand they walked back into the house. Nora was just setting the table with colorful Mexican plates. She looked up and smiled at them.

"It does my heart good to see Señor Walcott looking so happy."

"It feels good to have the woman I love next to me."

Guy pulled out a chair at the table and motioned for Lorraine to sit. She did and he put the cloth napkin in her lap.

"Bon apetit," he said as he sat down across the table from her.

Nora put enchiladas on their plates then left the room. They raised the glasses with red wine and nodded, smiling at each other.

"To us," he said

"To us," she echoed.

ഇഏഇ

The next morning over breakfast Guy asked her if she was ready to meet his children.

"I suppose I am. How many are there?"

"I doubt if all my children will be there, but you'll met at least some of them."

I have a feeling this is not what he wants me to think it is. I just can't imagine Guy spreading his seed all over the place. Not the way he has been with me. Maybe he just can't anymore, but what I felt last night with my back, I don't believe that.

"If you are agreeable, we'll spend the day in Old Town, have lunch in a wonderful restaurant, and, after school lets out, we'll go and see the children."

"Sounds good to me."

It was a sunny early August day with comfortable temperatures when they walked in the old main square of the city. There were art galleries, restaurants, and a variety of small shops with colorful merchandise. San Felipe de Neri Catholic Church was centered in a prominent location, like a patriarch keeping watch over his children.

"What a pretty church," Lorraine said, admiring the two bell towers. "The architecture looks like a combination of Southwest with European. Let's go inside."

They entered the cool, mostly whitewashed interior and took a seat in a pew near the front. After a short prayer, Lorraine said, "This is such a beautiful old church. I would love to get married here. Do you think that is feasible?"

"That would be okay with me, provided the priest does not have too many objections that I'm not Catholic."

"We'll just have to ask the priest how he feels about that," she said, giving him a pleading look.

"If that look asks me to become Catholic, the answer is no."

"Oh no, I wouldn't ask you to give up your faith. I respect yours and I hope you respect mine."

"That's a deal. Are you hungry enough for lunch?"

"Starting to be."

"Good, me too."

They stepped out into the warm sunshine and went into a cool restaurant where they enjoyed a leisurely lunch. Afterward, he drove into the inner city to a large building that looked like an old warehouse. Guy unlocked the door and they went in.

Sunshine streamed into the large open space. There were clusters of easels and clusters of an assortment of tables and chairs. The walls were covered with artwork obviously made by children. In one corner was a young woman cleaning easels and brushes, unaware that anyone had entered.

Guy and Lorraine approached her.

"Amy," Guy called.

The woman jumped, startled. "Guy, I didn't hear you come in." She put her work down and rushed over to hug him. "Welcome home, we missed you."

"Good to be back. You been holding down the fort? I

want you to meet my fiancée, Lorraine. Lorraine, this is my number one art teacher, Amy Kloss."

Lorraine reached out her hand and Amy took her fingertips. "Fiancée, well, well. Congratulations, Guy."

Lorraine studied the attractive, petite woman of about thirty with long straight black hair. *She's jealous. She was hoping to get Guy for herself.*

"In case you haven't figured out by now," Guy said, looking at Lorraine, "this is an art studio for children. They come here after school and paint and draw in all mediums. There are several teachers working for me. Schools keep cutting art and music due to budget cuts. I feel art and music are so important for child development, that I started this studio. A few of the children can afford to pay a small fee, but most of the kids can't. No one gets turned down as long as they keep up with their schoolwork. I have students from first to twelfth grade."

"And you call them your children," Lorraine said, delighted.

"Yes, they are my children in art. I'm even planning on expanding the program to include music. I have been talking with some music teachers about teaching here."

"And I want to tell you," said Amy, "that Guy finances this operation with mostly his own money."

"I got the idea when this old warehouse was for sale. I found out that the price was real low, so I figured there ought to be a good use for the building. That's when I came up with the idea. I believe money is to be in circulation. I have a good income, but now I also have a good outflow."

"I think this is wonderful. Oh, Guy, I really don't know what to say, only that I'm proud of you and—"

Before Lorraine could finish her thought, the outside door swung open and about twenty elementary school children ran in shouting, "Mr. Guy, you're back. Mr. Guy is back. We missed you."

Guy stooped down, extended his arms, and scooped up as many kids as his arms could hold. When they had their hug, the children made way for the others waiting for their embrace.

Watching the rapport Guy had with the children brought tears to Lorraine's eyes. Amy stood next to her and gave her a sideways glance. Lorraine saw the contempt in the woman's eyes. *I better watch out for her, she wants Guy for herself.*

Chapter 25

The next day the doctor's visit went well. Lorraine liked the middle-aged doctor. He was very personable and caring and she felt she was in good hands. The doctor examined her and told her that she had healed nicely and was able to resume all normal activity. When she came out with a big smile, Guy was sitting in the waiting room.

"All is well," she told him.

"That is great." He took her hand and walked with her to the car. "I wish we didn't have a commitment for this evening."

"I didn't know there was something going on tonight."

"Remember, I told you, there is a showing in the

warehouse of the children's art. Any art that is sold will go for the music program. All the children agreed to donate their work. I just have to be there. I understand there will be people from the symphony orchestra. I'm hoping they agree to donate some instruments. I hope you want to come, but I'm not forcing you. I expect just about all of my children will be there. I chose their best artwork for the sale."

"Yes, now I do remember. Of course, I'll go with you."

"Good, I want to introduce you around. This will be a totally different crowd than the one in Green Bay."

"In that case, is it formal?"

"No, tux and evening gowns not desired. Wear the slacks and blouse you are wearing right now, if you wish."

"Okay, Guy. I'm happy to go and eager to meet your friends. This is so exciting. I hope I can work and help you with the project, too."

"I'm sure there is some way you can help out. We'll talk about that later. Let's go home. There are a few things I need to take care of."

Hmm, I wonder what that might be. Are we going to make love today?

They got into his little blue sports car and drove back to the house.

When Lorraine saw Guy turn on his cell phone and head toward the garden, she knew that he did not have sex in mind. She headed for her room, picked up a novel, lay on the bed, and started reading. It was not long before she drifted off. Guy woke her up when supper was on the table.

ᗰᗰᗰ

When Lorraine and Guy arrived at the gallery, the place was packed with the young artists, their parents and friends, and some serious buyers. When the couple entered, people stopped their conversations, turned toward Guy and a smiling Lorraine, and clapped. Soon students and parents were gathered around Guy, pushing Lorraine to the side.

The one who started coming between them was Amy and an older woman who looked like she could be her mother.

That woman sure looks familiar. Where do I know her from? Oh no, it can't be her. Lorraine remembered a prison guard who was especially nasty. Suddenly, she started shaking. She went to the bathroom to compose herself.

While she was there, the older woman entered. She gave Lorraine an intense look and, with false sweetness, said, "The colors of black and white suit you a lot better than orange. You can't fool me. I know you from Perryville. I know you are a murderer. They should have never let you out."

Lorraine stared at the woman with her mouth open. She could not utter a sound.

"You damn black widow spider, how can you trap Guy in your net? He is way too good for the likes of you. I hope you rot in hell."

Two other women entered the ladies room, and the prison guard left abruptly. When the two women saw Lorraine looking distressed, one of them asked with genuine concern, "Are you all right, dear?"

"I'll be fine. I must have eaten something that didn't agree with me." Lorraine sat on one of the chairs. "I'll feel better soon, thank you. I'll just sit here a while."

"Want me to tell Guy you're not well?" the second woman asked.

"No, I'm starting to feel better already."

A few minutes later, Lorraine left the bathroom and saw the prison guard and Amy go throughout the room talking briefly with people. She saw people look at her and, when she caught their eyes, they quickly looked away. Meanwhile, Guy was engaged in deep conversation with the symphony orchestra conductor. Lorraine felt like leaving the building, but Guy had warned her that, under no circumstances, was she go out by herself as she did in Green Bay. He told her the warehouse was not in the best section of town. She went to the table with the punch bowl. A young teacher served her a cup of the non-alcoholic punch with a friendly smile. Soon, Amy walked up to the young woman and whispered in her ear and the warm smile became an icy, wide-eyed stare. Lorraine looked at Guy across the room and saw him give the conductor a big smile and handshake. *It looks like Guy just had a good meeting with the man.*

She walked over to Guy and asked him when he was planning on leaving.

"When the show is over in about an hour." Then he noticed the distress in her eyes. "Are you all right? You don't look well."

"I don't feel well."

"Then I'll take you home right now." He looked around the room and saw Amy. "Amy," he called as he waved. "I need to leave. Will you and Pedro close up the place when everyone leaves?"

"Sure, be glad to," she said with a knowing smile. "Will I see you tomorrow?"

"I expect you will. I have some money and checks, if there are any more, just take them home with you and bring them tomorrow to put in the bank."

"Don't worry. I'll take care of everything and I feel safe," she said, pointing to the prison guard. "My mother here is a professional guard."

"It's a pleasure meeting you, Mrs. Kloss."

"The pleasure's all mine," she answered sweetly.

Then Guy took Lorraine's hand and went out to the car.

While driving, Guy asked Lorraine what was hurting.

"I'll talk about it when we get home."

They drove the rest of the way in silence.

Once at home, Lorraine hurried into her room and closed the door. When Guy knocked on the door and asked if she was all right, she just told him that she would be out in a few minutes to talk. Meanwhile, he poured two glasses of white wine, put on some soft music, lit a few candles, then went into his bathroom to take a shower.

When Lorraine came out of her room, dressed in a kaftan, she was surprised by the romantic setting. She sat on the couch and stared at the two wine glasses sitting on the cocktail table as if they were crystal balls. Two glasses almost touching were like herself and Guy. She pictured a big space between them, just like she needed to get away from him. Guy came out of his room, wearing a dark paisley print silk robe. He sat next to her, took her hand, and kissed it.

"Now what is it you want to talk about?" he asked. "But first, let's drink a toast to ourselves."

"Oh, Guy, please don't make it any harder than it already is," Lorraine said with tears in her eyes. "But I need to get out of your life."

Without seeming surprised, Guy asked, "Why would you want to get out of my life? I thought you loved me as I love you."

"It's because I love you that I need to leave you. You are a successful artist and philanthropist. Having an ex-con in your life will hurt you. It will be better for you if I just quietly go away. You can have your choice of many women. They'll even be able to have your children. You don't need me."

"You're wrong, I do need you. Women throw themselves at me all the time. I don't love any of them. It's you, and only you, I love. When I first met you, bells went off in my head. I wanted nothing more than to make love to you. But I knew that making love leads to infatuation and that doesn't last long. I wanted to see if it's really love and, of that, I am totally sure. I want to spend the rest of my live with you."

"You probably didn't notice, but Amy's mother recognized me and she and Amy went around the room telling everyone that I am a murderer. I could see and feel the attitude toward me. It was not comfortable."

"I might not look like I'm aware of my surroundings, but I could feel the atmosphere in the room turn cold. I did not know the cause of it then, but I have a plan how we can turn that around."

"A plan? What could possibly salvage this situation?"

"I'll tell you if you promise you will not leave me, ever." He picked up the two wine glasses and handed one to her. "But first a toast to us."

Tears were running down her cheeks, but she smiled. "To us," she said, crying from sheer happiness.

They drank the wine and he took her in his arms and kissed her passionately.

"If you want to, just say so," she said.

"Want to what?"

"Being as you are sure this is real love...you know. I must tell you, I have not had a man for over fifteen years—"

He cut the sentence short with a passionate kiss. Suddenly, Lorraine's doubts and fears fled into the night. Here was a man who truly loved and wanted her as she loved and wanted him. The kiss was like a rose bud that manifested itself with the opening of its petals and expanding into a beautiful blossom that brought joy and pleasure to both of them.

After the first time, they both went into the master bedroom and again enjoyed the closeness of each other.

Chapter 26

The next morning, Lorraine could smell the bacon frying when she emerged from the bedroom wearing her kaftan. Guy was making breakfast. She sat at the granite top kitchen island and watched him skillfully manage the cooking. *He moves about the kitchen like a dancer. He makes love like a maestro playing the violin. Wow.* Just the thought made her body tingle.

"Good morning," she said, reaching for a mug of coffee.

"And a good morning it is, sweetheart." He leaned over and gave her a kiss. "We have a special day today."

"Oh, what is that?"

"I never did tell you my plan last night, and today we carry it out."

"What is your plan?"

"The feature editor of the newspaper is a friend of mine and he is coming over to interview you."

"Why, what is to gain?"

"Now that it is known that you have a record and were in jail, we will squelch the nasty rumors by telling the people the truth. You have to stop being ashamed of what you have been through and be proud of what you have overcome."

Her jaw dropped and it took a while before she could speak. "I never looked at it that way," she whispered.

"I read everything I could find about you," he said, putting two sunny eggs on her plate.

"Some of the newspaper articles even showed a little sympathy for you, the abused wife who stabbed the abuser in self-defense. It seems to me if you would have had a good lawyer, you would have gotten off." He saw tears in her eyes. "All I want to say is. be prepared to tell your side of the story. When we get done, you will be the hero."

"I did nothing heroic. The reason I survived is because I did not have the courage to kill myself. Believe me, there were times I felt like it. I just didn't have the opportunity."

"And I'm certainly glad you are here and now. In my eyes, you are a hero."

"Thank you" she whispered, and concentrated on her breakfast.

ℰℑℰℑ

Several hours later a car stopped at the curb and a young man emerged. Lorraine watched through the window as a very handsome man with short black hair headed toward the house. He carried a large camera and a notebook. From his gait, Lorraine could tell that the young man was of the gay persuasion. *Why is it the best looking men tend to be gay?*

After the door chimes rang, Guy opened the door and greeted his friend with a hug.

"And here is my beautiful fiancée Lorraine Lopez," Guy said, bringing the man into the living room. "This is my friend Buck Gianelli."

"It's a real pleasure meeting you," Lorraine said, reaching out her hand.

"I heard a lot about you," Buck said, giving her a warm hug. "Let me begin by getting a few pictures. Some of you alone and some with Guy."

After he photographed them, he put the camera away, opened his notebook, and started asking questions. He also talked with Guy about his art studio for the children and his plans to expand it into music. After two hours Buck closed his notebook. "I'm going to write this article when I get to the office. If it's not in tomorrow's *Journal*, it most likely will be the day after. This will make a terrific story. Thank you so much for giving me the opportunity to write this."

"I'm the one to thank you, Buck."

"And don't forget to let me know when you set the wedding date."

"We will," Guy assured him while walking him to the door. "Till next time. Hope we do lunch or dinner together soon."

"I'll be out of town next week. Let you know when I get back."

Guy had his arm over Lorraine's shoulder as they watched Buck leave. "I can tell from his demeanor that he is lonely. I hope Buck finds a partner, too."

"He looks very happy and outgoing to me," Lorraine said. "What makes you think he's lonely?"

"I don't know exactly. It must be just some little motions he is not even aware of. I am fine-tuned to emotions."

"I suppose no one can get away with lying to you."

"Mostly not, but occasionally one slips through." he said firmly.

"I hate liars, too. I promise to never lie to you."

"Me too. I won't lie to you either."

They sealed the promise with a kiss then spent the afternoon exploring more of their new-found pleasure.

ოჳ

The next day, the feature section of the *Albuquerque Journal* had a full page article about Guy Walcott and his amazing fiancée. It showed Lorraine in the light of a victim who, in desperation and self-defense, killed her abuser. It explained about her unfair trial and fifteen years in prison. She used that time to learn a valuable skill and came out a better person. It also mentioned how they met, and their trip to Austin for her to donate a kidney for her daughter. The article concluded with the writer wishing them happiness.

The phone did not stop ringing that day and the next few days. Cards and letters of admiration poured in for Lorraine. Neighbors brought over enough cakes and goodies for them to open a bakery. So as not to waste any of it, the treats were brought to the studio for the children. Then checks arrived for Guy's art and music programs, along with donations of used instruments.

"I have never been happier in my life," Guy said to Lorraine while they were in the garden, watching the hummingbirds at the feeders. "And I owe it all to you."

"You are the amazing person. I am so proud of what you are doing and can't wait to be your wife."

"How are the wedding plans coming?"

"We have some openings at San Felipe de Neri to consider. The priest will marry us if we go to a premarital counseling with him."

"What is a celibate man going to tell us that we don't know better?"

"He just wants to have it in his mind that we are good for each other."

"Okay, make a date with him, and I'll be there."

"Thank you, Guy."

He took her hand and kissed it. "Now this little silver band needs to be replaced with a proper engagement ring."

"I had a big engagement ring the last time. I like the silver ring. Use that money for something more useful."

"My dear frugal Lorraine. I will get you a nice wedding band though. Have you any wish for a honeymoon?"

"I had not even thought about it. Just being with you is honeymoon enough."

"In that case, I'll pick the destination. Okay with you?"

"Okay with me."

Chapter 27

The wedding was set for the Saturday of Labor Day weekend. Lorraine had booked several rooms in a hotel near the church. On Thursday both Rachel and her sister Maria arrived. To Lorraine's surprise, they came with Elena and Juan in their Cadillac. Lorraine met them in the hotel lobby and cried with joy on seeing both of her daughters. She held them in an embrace as if she never wanted to let go. Even Elena and Juan gave her warm hugs. All the hatred and resentment from the past had been released.

"We wish you much joy and happiness," said Juan, her former father-in-law.

"And that goes for me too," Elena said. "It was you who saved Rachel's life. How are you doing?"

"Thank you, I'm well. Don't miss the kidney one little bit."

"Juan, let's go to our room and drop off our suitcase, then I want to do some sightseeing," Elena said. "Come, Juan, time to go."

"*Sí*, Elena, *hasta la vista*," he said as they headed toward the elevator.

"Let's go up to my suite, we have too many years to catch up on," Lorraine suggested. "We can order lunch in."

"That's great, Mom," said Rachel. "I still have to be careful not to get exposed to too many people and germs"

Once they entered the room, Lorraine asked both girls to stand there and she took a few steps back. "I just want to look at the most beautiful sight in the world. My two beautiful daughters standing in front of me and looking happy. You definitely look like sisters. You did inherit your father's good looks and almost black hair. Your large green eyes give your face an almost exotic look." Lorraine went to them and again embraced them. "I just can't get enough of the feel of you, my two beautiful daughters. There were times I thought I would never ever see you again."

"What are the plans for the wedding?" Maria asked.

"As you know, you two are my only bridesmaids. Let me see what you are wearing."

Both girls opened their suitcases and pulled out gowns. Rachel's was red with a V-line neck and a full chiffon skirt. Maria's was the same style in royal blue.

"They are beautiful, and you could not have picked better. It is as if you knew which dress I would pick for myself." She went to the closet and brought out a white silk dress of similar styling.

"Tomorrow, I'm expecting Frank and Kimberly and the two boys along with my mom. It would be perfect if Jaime could come too, but he is so far away in Annapolis."

Lorraine did not notice the girls exchanging glances and smiles. "It will be good seeing Grandma, Uncle Frank, and Aunt Kim and meeting the cousins, but remember," Rachel reminded her, "I need to keep my distance. Now is there going to be a reception and where?"

"You know, I don't know. It was going to be a very small wedding, but Guy is a celebrity and the small quickly grew. I just ended up getting a wedding planner and left everything in her hands. Most of the events will be a total surprise to me. I think Guy knows more than I do."

"When are we going to meet Mr. Wonderful?" Maria asked.

"Tonight. We'll have a rehearsal at church."

"On a Thursday already?" Rachel commented.

"Yes, tomorrow night there is another wedding at the church. That gives us time to have a family dinner at a private room in a restaurant."

"Does Guy have any family?" Maria wanted to know.

"He does have some aunts, uncles, and cousins. They live out of town and I won't meet them until tomorrow also."

"Sounds like it will be a big dinner. Just let me sit in a corner with Maria and my grandparents provided they are invited."

"Of course they are. After all, they're family," Lorraine said with a choking voice.

Rachel gave her mom a hug. "Are you all right?"

"Better than all right. There was a time I thought I would never be in the same room with the Lopezes, and now we are celebrating together—my wedding no less. I did not realize until now what a heavy burden hate and resentment can be. Truly now, that millstone has been released from around my neck and I feel light and happy. Life could not be better—well, yes, one little thing. If only Jaime could be here. He said he would call on Saturday. I will just have be to content with that."

Lorraine and her two daughters had spent the two nights before the wedding in the hotel suite. On Saturday morning they rose early and had breakfast in the room. Then hairdressers came and styled the women's hair. Lorraine's had some length and blond highlights. The only ornament in the curls of Lorraine's neck-length hair was a comb of small silk-and-pearl roses. When the hairdressers completed the make-up, they left. The girls helped their mother put on her long ivory silk dress with a V-neckline and a full A-line skirt. They stood back with awe.

"Mom, you look absolutely gorgeous," Rachel said.

"And I have the two most beautiful daughters in the world," Lorraine said, looking at the two wearing the bright red and royal blue dresses. "We definitely look like the all-American girls."

"Now we need the photographer," Maria said, dialing a number on her cell phone.

A few minutes later there was a knock on the door. Rachel opened it and let in two young men. One of them was carrying a professional camera. The second was wearing a uniform. Lorraine did not look at the men to begin with. It was only when she posed with her daughters that she paid attention to the men.

She saw the double row of gold buttons on the black jacket and slowly raised her eyes.

When she came to the face, she let out a yell. "Jaime, it is you. How wonderful." She lunged forward and embraced the young man. "You came, how simply wonderful," she said, kissing him on the cheeks. "Now the family picture is complete. I'm so happy I feel like crying, but I can't mess up the mascara."

"It's waterproof," Maria said.

"You girls knew all along, didn't you?"

"We did not know for sure until he called from the airport," Rachel said. "Grandma and Grandpa Lopez picked him up."

"We better get to church," Lorraine said. "The family will be in a private room. They will all be most eager to see our dear Jim."

Everyone left the hotel, expecting to ride in a limo the short way to church. However behind a white limo stood a landau carriage drawn by two white horses. The charioteer took Lorraine's hand and helped her into the black coach decorated with flowers. The two girls joined her there. Jaime and the photographer rode to church in the limousine. When the carriage pulled up in front of the church, the bells in the two bell towers were ringing. People stood outside cheering and applauding while the bride emerged from the carriage. Lorraine looked around at all the smiling faces. *Are these people all here for me and Guy? Maybe there is someone famous in town that I am not aware of.*

The whole family was in a side room waiting for her. Soon the ushers, who were friends of the groom, came to escort Mary Albright and the Lopezes to their seats.

"Jim, I was going to walk down the aisle alone, but now that you are here, would you walk with me?"

"Mom, I would be honored to," he said, offering his left arm.

The organ was playing while the two bridesmaids walked down the aisle with two groomsmen. When Jonathan Cain's "Bridal March" was played, Lorraine stepped out into the filled-to-capacity church. The pews were decorated with white flowers and green leaves. Four large baskets of white flowers adorned the altar. Lorraine looked at the bridal bouquet of red roses surrounding a white orchid. The bouquet looked like it was shimmying.

"Relax Mom, everything is well."

"It is all so beautiful, I can't believe it. The best part is that you and the girls are here."

"Just take some deep breaths, take your time, every-one will wait."

Lorraine stood there for a good minute, calming her-self. Then she saw Guy, dressed in a black tuxedo with tails, standing at the altar patiently waiting.

"Let's go Jim. I have someone waiting to marry me."

Slowly they walked down the aisle while the music was playing. Lorraine saw many wet eyes and she did not even know the people.

After the vows, Guy slipped a ring on her finger. It contained three half-carat round diamonds and baguettes intermingled in a twist. Then there was a shy kiss while people clapped and the newlyweds walked down the aisle and got into the carriage. The carriage took a leisurely ride through the city to the delight of everyone on the street. Finally, they arrived at the reception. It was being held in the art studio that had been transformed into a wedding wonderland with drapes on the walls and tables with red, white, and blue flowers as centerpieces. One wall was covered from the high ceiling to the floor with art work by the children. Most of them were wedding themes.

Against one wall was a long elevated table for the wedding party and family that included Mr. and Mrs. Lopez. Wait staff served food and drinks. While everyone was eating, a string quartet played music and, occasionally, two singers sang romantic songs. Some songs were solos and others duets.

Guy leaned over to his wife. "Those are my aunt and uncle. They sang with the opera."

Most, if not all, of Guy's art children were there. All of the girls were dressed in white dresses. Any girls that did not have a white dress or could not afford to buy one, received money for one. The boys wore white shirts and dark pants. The children assembled in front of the VIP table and sang "More Than You'll Ever Know" to the delight of everyone present.

"That is the first presentation of the music program," Guy said with pride.

"That is wonderful. Oh Guy, I can't believe what a day this is turning out to be. I have never been happier in my life."

"This is just the beginning of the very happy rest of your life." He took her face in his hands and kissed her on the lips.

Everyone in the room cheered and hollered, "Kiss her again," and he did.

Not only did a Mariachi band play for dancing, but a master of ceremonies led in mixers and getting acquainted dances. Before long, everyone in the room was up dancing. It was late at night before exhaustion took over and people slowly left the party. Even the bride and groom stayed until most people had left. Then the two went to Guy's house and celebrated behind closed doors.

Chapter 28

The next day, Lorraine's family gathered at Guy's house. There were Lorraine's three children, her mother, and brother Frank and his family, Juan and Elena Lopez. Everyone gathered around the large dining room table and did a needed job. There were hundreds of wedding cards to be opened and read. When someone had a card with a special hand written message, that person would read it aloud to everyone. Many cards contained cash and checks, all for the art and music studio. Any monetary donation was immediately acknowledged with a thank you note written by the bride, her two daughters, Kimberly, her mother Mary, and Elena.

Guy signed each one with only his first name. "I'm glad my name is short, I'm getting writer's cramps."

After a few hours, that job was done and the notes were ready to mail. About that time Nora had prepared her Mexican specialty of *chilorio* with rice and salads and served it.

"Mom, Guy, are you going on a honeymoon?" Rachel asked.

Lorraine looked questionably at Guy.

"Yes, we are taking the last cruise of the summer to Alaska. I hope that is agreeable with you?" he said, looking at his wife.

"Wonderful, I have never been on a cruise."

"You'll love it," Jaime assured her. "I find being on the ocean very spiritual."

"We'll sail out of Seattle in a few days. I went all out and booked the best room on the ship. This will be our opportunity to totally get away. We don't even have to leave the suite if we don't want to."

Lorraine laughed. "If I know you, you'll be climbing all over the ship."

"I probably will."

"I hate to break up this family gathering," Jaime said, "but in about one hour I need to leave for the airport and catch my red-eye back to Baltimore."

"Baltimore?" Maria said. "I thought the Academy is in Annapolis."

"It is, but Baltimore is the closest airport. I hope you all will get a chance to visit me there."

"We'll plan on it," Juan said, "if not before, we'll certainly make it for graduation."

"Just be sure you rent a place well ahead of time," Jaime warned.

"I think it's really cool and all you going to the Academy." said Jeremy, the cousin. "I would like to go there too. Will you help me get in?"

"I have absolutely no say who gets in," Jaime answered. "All I can tell you is get good grades, participate in athletics, be a good citizen, and get a nomination from a member of congress. Then the hard job is staying in. About one in four drop out, most in the first year."

"Jeremy does get good grades and plays sports," his mother, Kimberly, chimed in.

"I'll be glad to give you a ride to the airport," Frank said. "Tomorrow we'll drive back to Phoenix. Now that we have gotten re-acquainted, would you include us in your contacts?"

"I certainly will, Uncle Frank and Aunt Kimberly and you cousins. We have too many lost years to make up for."

Then Juan Lopez rose and looked each person at the table before he spoke. "Family, yes we are a family again. Mary, Elena, and I have three grandchildren borne by Lorraine with our son, Alexandro, may God rest his soul. It took us a long time to see that our son had bad faults, and, unfortunately, that caused his tragic demise. Lorraine suffered harshly because of it. I too must confess that I carried the curse of hate in me for too many years. I hated you, Mary, even though you had nothing to do with it. I hated Lorne who was a kind and gentle man who died all too young, as a result of what had happened. I hated you Frank and your family, just because you are an Albright. I love you, my three grandchildren, and thought of you as my own. I even had you call us Mom and Dad. That is no longer so, we are your grandparents or if you wish you can call me *Abuelo* and your grandmother *Abuela*. I too have released the burden of hate and resentment. I am happy for you, Lorraine, that you have found such a fine man to marry. Elena and I wish both of you many years of happiness. There is a beautiful saying in Spanish that is *Salud, dinero y amor y tiempo para disfrutarlos.* For those that don't know, it means good health, wealth, and love and the time to enjoy it. I hope you have a hundred years or more to enjoy each other." He raised his glass of wine. "*Salud.*"

Everyone else raised their glasses of wine, beer, iced tea, and soda and said, "*Salud.*"

Then Mary Albright stood up, looked at everyone, and spoke. "That was beautiful, Juan. You said it just about all. I too released the resentment I felt so many years toward you both. The past is gone and cannot be changed, but what we do in the present affects the future. Now this family has a future of love and understanding. It does my heart good to have a relationship with the Lopez clan, and we welcome with open arms our newest family member, Guy Walcott." Looking at her daughter and Guy holding hands, she continued. "May your love for each other multiply with the years. I only wish your father could be with us now."

"Mom, somehow I feel he is in this room at this very moment. I have been feeling his presence for the past two days."

"I hope you're right, my child."

"My child. It has been decades since I have heard that term. Mom, I'm proud to be your child."

"Thank you, Lorraine, and I'm proud to be your mother."

"I think I better go and get my rubber boots," Frank said. "The syrup is getting a bit thick."

"Frank, behave yourself," Mary reprimanded. "I love and am proud of you and your family. You have always been there for me."

She raised her glass and cheerfully saluted the newlyweds and everyone else. Everyone followed suit.

After an hour, the guests had all departed. While Nora cleared the table and took care of the dishes, Guy and Lorraine stepped out into the garden.

"What a weekend this has been," Lorraine said with a sigh. "The last time I had that much drama, it was all negative. This has all been good and positive. There was a time I thought I would never be happy again. Oh, Guy, now I feel I will burst with sheer happiness."

"Now I don't want you exploding, but I do want you to remain happy."

The doorbell rang and Nora answered it. She came out into the garden with Sami in her arm. "Sami, come to Mommy."

The little dog ran toward Lorraine, jumped into her arms, and licked her face and neck.

"Sami, you dear little critter, I had almost forgotten him in the excitement. Frank did ask if he should bring him, and I never even asked about him. Oh you poor little Sami, were you in the hotel all that time?"

"I'm sure he was better off there, than with all the excitement. He is here now, and that is all that matters." Guy reached for her hand and put it to his lips. "We are together and we will always be."

"Yes, you are my immediate family and I have my extended family again. What more could I want?"

"I know I have everything I need right here." Guy rose and led her into the house.

Sami jumped up on a chair in the garden and closed his eyes. His face appeared to smile.

THE END

About the Author

When Ellynore Seybold-Smith was just a kid, she knew she wanted to be a writer. Her first book, *The Wooden Mistress*, was published in 1994. Then in 2012, Smith was diagnosed with cancer. She thought, if it was time to die, okay. After all, her husband was waiting on the other side. Then a miracle happened, and the tumor turned benign. Smith saw this as a message from God that she had better do something creative with the rest of her life. And she began to write in earnest.

www.ingramcontent.com/pod-product-compliance
Lightning Source LLC
Chambersburg PA
CBHW060733180626
46819CB00001B/7